All I Want For Christmas Is You

SUSANA ELLIS

Copyright © 2023. All rights reserved to © Barbara Andrews, writing as Susana Ellis.

All I Want For Christmas Is You is licensed for your personal enjoyment only and may not be resold or given away to other people. If you would like to share this book, please purchase an additional copy for each recipient. If you're reading this book and did not purchase it, or it was not purchased for your use only, then please return to your favorite retailer and purchase your own copy. Thank you for respecting the hard work of these authors.

All rights reserved. No part of this book may be reproduced in any form or by any means without the prior written consent of the author of that part, except for including brief quotations in a review. Names, characters, and incidents depicted in this book are products of the author's imagination or are used in a fictitious situation. Any resemblances to actual events, locations, organizations, incidents, or persons—living or dead—are coincidental and beyond the intent of the author.

Cover Design by Aileen Fish

ePub: ISBN: 978-1-945503-10-8

Print ISBN: 978-1-945503-11-5

This story originally appeared in *Christmastide Kisses*, a Bluestocking Belles with Friends collection, published in 2023.

 Created with Vellum

Foreword

ALL I WANT FOR CHRISTMAS IS YOU

Alicia's story begins in *The Third MacPherson Sister*, where her unkindness results in Rebecca MacPherson's unceremonious removal from London. But the spoiled duke's daughter suffers repercussions as well, and for the first time she yearns to be a better person. Perhaps the handsome young vicar might be able to help her.

Evan and Alicia are strongly attracted to each other, but she's not for him. Her wealth and status—and his past—stand between them. What will it take for this pair to realize that love is the only thing that matters?

Chapter One

19 December 1817
Residence of the Duke of Huntingdon
Mayfair, London

"Must you always be badgering me on this matter, Wife? Alicia is barely one-and-twenty. She and Stanton will settle down one of these days. I daresay they are on the brink of setting a date even as we speak."

The duke's young wife crossed her arms in front of her chest. "So you've told me for the last two years. Not only have they *not* set a date, Lucas, but they rarely even *see* each other! Alicia has danced more with the Prince Regent than with her own betrothed this past Season!"

The Duke of Huntingdon closed his book and laid his spectacles on top of it. "Has that old lecher been philandering with my girl? I'll see him in hell first!"

Cheeks flushed, the young duchess clenched her fists. "No, of course not! That's not the point, and you know it well. What I've been trying to tell you is that Alicia and Milton Gardiner show no signs of partiality for each other's company, and people are beginning to question whether the marriage will ever be accomplished at all!"

Her eyes narrowed. "The Prince danced as many times with *me* this Season, but you've never said a word against him. I believe you care for *her* more than your own wife!"

She pulled out a handkerchief and swiped it over her eyes.

The duke rolled his eyes. "Good God, Elise, must you always make a fuss about everything? You know very well that as an unmarried young woman, Alicia's reputation must be spotless, or no one, not even Stanton, will marry her. She and Stanton have always been the best of friends. Neither has ever spoken a word against their childhood betrothal, and you know Alicia well enough to know that she would certainly do so if she wished to." He snorted.

"As for Stanton, he can hardly be expected to dance with the gel when he's spent most of the Season in Norfolk taking over his father's duties on the estate. It may be unfashionable for a young man to take his responsibilities seriously, but I say it speaks well of his character."

Lady Huntingdon glared at him. "And when Blackburn dies, the wedding will be postponed a year at least. Lucas, I must insist that you speak to your daughter immediately and impress upon her the urgency of securing this marriage as soon as may be!"

* * *

At the sound of her stepmother's footsteps moving toward the door, Alicia fled down the hall into the nearest room where she posed in front of the hearth and pretended to be studying a portrait of her late mother. Too late, she thought better of the idea. Elise hated that portrait of her predecessor almost as much as she hated Alicia herself.

The staccato clicks of her stepmother's heels on the wooden floor paused when they passed the drawing room where Alicia had taken refuge.

"What are you doing here?" Elise demanded, her voice dripping with suspicion.

Alicia shrugged and smiled innocently. "Why, looking at my mother's portrait, of course."

The duchess's brow furrowed. "Were you eavesdropping on my conversation with your father?"

Alicia's mouth assumed a slack expression. "Were you having a conversation with my father? About me?"

Her stepmother's nostrils flared. "You *were* listening! I knew it!" she snapped. "Did you learn anything interesting?"

"I-I, well...," Alicia stammered.

One of the upstairs maids appeared in the doorway, looking worried.

"A thousand pardons, your grace, but you're needed in the nursery. Master Gervase is poorly today, and Nurse wishes to call in a physician."

"Gervase, my darling child... ill? Oh my, I knew that Nurse should not have taken him out of doors yesterday! Oh, I must go to him immediately!"

She gave Alicia a menacing stare, lifted her skirts, and rushed toward the stairway.

The maid winked at Alicia. "More 'n likely he's just teething." Then she took off after her mistress.

Alicia sighed heavily and gazed up at her mother's beautiful face. It was almost like looking in a mirror, as she had inherited Frances Howland's dark wavy hair, tawny eyes, and high cheekbones. Her prominent nose and light brown skin that no amount of lemon juice scrubs would lighten had come from her father, who had some French ancestry in his blood.

"Oh Mama! Why did you have to go sailing *that* day, of all days?"

She pressed her face down against the cool marble surface of the mantel. Three years ago she'd received the devastating news that her mother and Lady Blackburn had drowned when the skiff they'd been sailing had run into a sudden storm and capsized in the Wash a mile off the Norfolk coast. Her life had never been the same since. Particularly not when, after a year of mourning, her father had married a young girl only a few years older than she, who'd had the nerve to bear him the son he'd always wanted soon after.

Her new stepmother, the daughter of a baronet whose mother claimed to be a displaced French countess, had been scheming to get rid of Alicia from the first day she'd moved in. Alicia was a constant reminder of her mother, a notorious London beauty. Elise's skin was the pale porcelain favored by society, but in combination with her gray eyes, small round head and pale blonde hair, she tended to fade into the woodwork. With dark hair in fashion these days, it galled her to appear in public with the stepdaughter who outshone her.

Nor did it help when all the servants showed a pronounced preference for Alicia.

"That's not my fault," she said lifting her head to her mother's face as if to defend her behavior. "I never encouraged them to do that."

But you never did anything to prevent it, did you, Daughter? You weren't raised to prevaricate, you know. This type of behavior is beneath you.

A lump formed in Alicia's throat. It was true. Her mother, at least, had worked very hard to keep her grounded in good Christian values and a healthy respect for others. Alicia knew her mother would have been sorely distressed to see the way she provoked her stepmother, sometimes without half-trying.

Your behavior causes your father much grief, you know. Does he not deserve a peaceful home?

Alicia paled as she recalled the conversation she'd just overheard in her father's study. Unkind as it was to deliberately provoke her stepmother, it also had the effect of disturbing her father's domestic life. Which she'd not hesitated to do at first when she'd been furious with her father's decision to remarry, but now... it seemed rather childish and cruel.

He's been a good father to you, Alicia. He was a good husband to me as well. Does he not deserve your loyalty?

"Alicia, my dear."

Lucas Howland, the Duke of Huntingdon, strolled through the doorway toward her. At forty-nine, he was still a fine figure of a man, although his dark hair was now sprinkled with gray and his stomach was beginning to make itself known beneath his olive-green waistcoat.

He sighed as he cupped her shoulders and drew her against his chest as they both gazed up at the portrait of his first wife.

"Aye, she was a marvelous woman. I still miss her too, you know. Many times I wish I had forbidden her to take the boat out that day."

Tears gathered in Alicia's eyes. "But she would never have heeded you, Papa. It wasn't your fault."

He turned her around and hugged her to his chest. "No, she was a willful one, my Frances. So spirited and full of life... I'm sure it never occurred to her that it could all be lost so quickly and tragically."

They stood there a moment and reflected on what the loss of the former duchess had brought to their lives. For the duke—a young second wife and the heir he'd always wanted. For Alicia—a new baby brother with whom she'd felt an instant connection, but who came with the inconvenience of an antagonistic stepmother.

"She was my best friend," Alicia whispered. "I could tell her anything and she would never laugh at me or remonstrate with me. She always told me to forget the past and live each day to the fullest."

She lifted her wounded face to her father's. "But how can I forget *her*? She was my life and now she's gone! I feel... lost without her, Papa."

Her father sighed and kissed her forehead before drawing her head to his shoulder. "I know it well, my dear. I've seen you drift aimlessly through two Seasons, and I know well things would have been much different had it been your mother sponsoring you and not your aunt."

"Aunt Tabitha has been very kind, Papa, but you are correct—it's not the same."

Her father's sister had not got on well with her sister-in-law and it seemed Alicia had inherited too many of her mother's characteristics to make for an amicable connection between aunt and niece.

The duke turned and, taking her arm, led her to a settee.

"Come and sit with me, Daughter. It's been a long time since we've spoken privately, and I think a chat is quite overdue. Shall I order tea?"

Tea? Alicia forced herself to relax her hands, which had tightened into fists at her father's request. She knew where this conversation was going.

"No tea, Papa. It will be time for nuncheon soon. I suppose you want to know about how things stand between Milton and me."

Her father patted her hand. "I don't wish to push you out of the nest, Alicia, but people are beginning to wonder if you and Stanton mean to marry after all. You've had two Seasons and I've heard no reports of your forming any other attachments in that time."

Because everyone knows I've been betrothed to Milton forever.

"I had beaux," she said defensively. "I was never a wallflower, you know. I had any number of escorts to Vauxhall and drives through the park."

The duke heaved a sigh. "Of course, you did. I never meant to imply otherwise. But of all of them, did none appeal to you as a better choice for husband than young Stanton?"

"No, nothing like that." Well, there was Lord Hadley, the handsome young viscount who made all the young ladies' hearts flutter, but he'd gone off on his Grand Tour last year and showed no sign of returning any time soon.

"As far as I know, Papa, Milton and I still plan to be married. I haven't heard from him lately, since he's been so busy at Blackburn, but I'm sure we'll discuss very soon."

Her father grimaced. "I don't mean to pressure you, my dear, but with Blackburn's illness, you might want to set an early date. I'm sure it would give him great pleasure to see his son wed before... well, there's no way to avoid the fact that his days are numbered."

"And once he's gone, there will be a year of mourning. I do realize that, Papa. I'm sure Elise will be no end of piqued to have me on your hands for another year."

Her father flinched. "It's not that, Alicia. It's just that... it's obvious you're not happy with us, and we think it's time you settled down and started your own family. With Stanton, if he's your choice. No one wishes to force you out, least of all your stepmother."

Alicia snorted. Did her father really think she would believe that? She'd have known it to be an untruth even if she had not overheard their recent conversation.

"Of course not. I'm sure Elise is eager to become a grandmother."

Her father tried to hide his grin, and Alicia turned and gave him a quick kiss on the cheek.

"I'll discuss it with Milton, Papa. He has a lot on his mind these days. When his father dies, he'll be alone in the world. At least I still have a father left."

Her father let out a huge breath. "Thank you, my dear."

He stood and started to leave, then turned and looked at her with a twinkle in his eye.

"I can't speak for Elise, of course, but I for one am looking forward to becoming a grandfather with great anticipation. And I'm sure Gervase will be in alt to have a little niece or nephew to play with."

Alicia blushed. "Really, Papa!"

Baby Gervase an uncle? An amusing image, but it all seemed so premature. She'd been betrothed to Milton for so long, but the actual marriage had seemed far off. In all that time, she'd never actually thought much about being Milton's wife and having his children. Now that the time seemed imminent, she felt a growing feeling of panic. Bridal nerves, of course. All brides had them. It would all turn out well in the end, she assured herself.

* * *

30 November 1817
The Vicarage
Castle Acre, Norfolk

The Reverend Evan Campbell closed his book—a doctrinal treatise he was using to plan his Sunday sermon—and set it down on the bench next to him. Gazing sightlessly at the weathered gravestones in the churchyard, he wondered for the umpteenth time when his sister would be returning home. He was seriously concerned that she had become embroiled in a most unsuitable situation, but she most uncharacteristically refused to speak about it, and seeing as she was of age—at twenty-five, a year older than he—he wasn't sure what to do about it.

Sighing, he focused on a small flat memorial plaque in front of the "reflecting bower" where he liked to sit and either work on sermons or contemplate the meaning of life. Perhaps he should have resolved the latter already, having embarked on a career as a vicar, but he was well aware that the pious figure he presented to the public was a façade. Deep inside, Evan retained innumerable doubts as to his calling and his fitness as a servant of God.

Mary Fuller
1629 - 1645
There is therefore now no condemnation to them which are in Christ Jesus, who walk not after the flesh, but after the Spirit.

Sixteen years old. What could she have done to earn such an

epitaph? Had she died of some malady, he thought it likely her gravestone would have been inscribed with something more sentimental, like *Rest in Peace* or *Love is Eternal*. But whoever Mary's loved ones had been, they had paid significantly more to have inscribed a longer scriptural message that seemed to indicate she had done something quite dreadful in her short lifetime. Was she a thief or a murderer? Birthed a child out of wedlock? Even during the Civil War, with Cromwell's puritanical leanings, such a moral lapse was not punishable by death. Childbirth, of course, offered its own hazards to women, whether virtuous or not.

He bit his lip as the image of his sister Ellen came to mind. She'd always been the sensible one, grounded in her faith and always there to rein him in during his wilder, rebellious days. In all truth, *she* was the one who insisted he had it in him to be a spiritual leader. He wasn't at all certain, even now, a year after being entrusted with the living at Castle Acre Parish.

And now he feared that *she* was the one in danger of serious moral lapse.

It all started two months ago when they'd traveled to Swaffham on some errands and settled down for a meal at the Suckling Pig Inn. John and Helen Green, a middle-aged couple from his parish, stopped by to greet them, and Mrs. Green happened to mention that an experienced nurse was urgently needed at Blackburn, a few miles up the road, near King's Lynn.

"When his lordship the earl took sick last spring, my sister was brought in to nurse him—her late husband was a doctor, you know—but her daughter in Norfolk is laid up with a broken limb and needs someone to help her with the four boys. Rapscallions, the lot of them."

Evan and Ellen listened politely as Mrs. Green chatted about her niece's good-for-nothing husband and how it was entirely his fault the boys had turned out to be unmanageable, and Evan tried not to think about their beefsteak pies fresh from the oven that had begun to cool and congeal on their plates.

At long last, Mrs. Green came to the point, and turned her

gaze toward Ellen. "I understand that Miss Campbell here is an accomplished nurse, after nursing your mother for several years. Might you be interested in the position, my dear?"

Ellen swallowed and shook her head quickly. "I thank you for thinking of me, Mrs. Green, but as you know, I am quite busy managing my brother's household and ministry. I couldn't possibly abandon him."

Mr. Green coughed and looked longingly at the doorway as his wife waved a hand in dismissal.

"As you know, my daughter Celia is quite accomplished in the housewifely arts. I'm sure she could manage to replace you for as long as it takes his lordship to go aloft to meet the Creator."

She leaned forward and patted Ellen on the shoulder, forestalling the protests that rose to the lips of one—and possibly both—Campbells. "Your commitment to your brother is much to your credit, my dear, but do you not think it is past time for you both to seek your separate fortunes? Why, the vicar here is unquestionably in need of a wife, and frankly, my dear, it is past time you yourself were settled."

Evan could see Ellen's cheeks burning and her eyes flashing daggers in Mrs. Green's direction, so he squeezed her hand under the table and gave her a warning look.

"I'm sure my sister and I are very grateful for your concern, but we are quite satisfied with our present situation."

Mrs. Green's transparent scheme to make a match for her daughter with the young unmarried vicar was not the first Evan had faced in his two years as a minister. Experience, though, hadn't made it any easier to remove himself from such situations without causing ruffled feathers and acrimony in the congregation.

In the end, Mrs. Green trumped his protests by playing the "vicar's duty" card. The very least he could do as a man of God was to visit the ailing earl and ensure that his physical and spiritual needs were being met.

"Blackburn has its own vicar," fumed Ellen as they set off

down Narborough Road in the dogcart Evan used to make his calls. "Why should *you* take on the responsibility for the earl?"

Evan shrugged. "I only agreed to visit the earl," he assured her. "Not to the rest of her plans. Sometimes it's best to concede the battle and win the war. Besides, the vicar in East Winch parish is away on leave and asked me to assist his curate." He grinned. "It's a duty visit, nothing more. No need to worry that you'll get inveigled into becoming the earl's nurse. I know well how hard you travailed to nurse Mama through her last illness, Ellen. All you have to do is refuse."

But as soon as she saw Milton Gardiner, the thought of refusing seemed to have flown right out of Ellen's mind.

She tried to tell her brother on the way home that the condition of the ailing earl had touched her heart and that it was only a temporary position until an older woman could be found, but he knew it was the earl's handsome son Milton, Viscount Stanton, who was responsible for changing her mind.

The moment they'd locked eyes on one another, both had turned quiet, flushed, and then smiled at each other. Evan knew that silly grin, having seen it on his cronies when they caught a glimpse of a comely wench. He wasn't sure what had occurred in his absence while he did his pastoral duty with the aged earl, but when he returned to the drawing room, they moved apart quickly on the settee where they sat next to each other and there was a guilty look in his sister's eyes when she looked at him.

Oh God! Ellen had fallen for a man well above her social circle. A man known to be betrothed, to boot.

The conversation on the way home had been intense.

"It's one thing to nurse our mother, Ellen, but for a young unmarried woman to take on the care of a gentleman—it's simply not done and you know it!"

Ellen's jaw was set.

"It's my Christian duty to help others, Evan. And it's only until a new nurse can be hired. I nursed Papa too, you know, in his last days. Only the most narrow-minded gossipmongers would cavil about the vicar's spinster sister nursing someone in need."

Evan glared at her and narrowly avoided directing the horses into a ditch. "Damn it, Ellen, it's not the old man that's the problem and you know it! It's not proper for you to be spending so much time in a house with young Stanton in it! Can you tell me truthfully that he's not the attraction here?"

Ellen folded her arms across her chest. "It's only for the day, Evan. I'll be coming home every night. And Milton—that is, Lord Stanton—won't be in the house that often. Just for meals, really. He's been helping one of his neighbors with a drainage project."

Evan gave deep sigh. They were *already* on a first-name basis? That wasn't like his level-headed sister at all.

"But it *is* Stanton. I saw the way you looked at each other! Ellen, he's promised to another woman!"

"I know that. He told me. It doesn't matter." Her tone was unconvincing.

Evan's muscles tensed. "I'm not a fool, Ellen. I saw the way you two looked at each other. There's more to this than a Christian desire to help the needy. I can't allow you to fall into the depths of temptation like this. It would be reckless and negligent for me to do so."

Ellen rammed her elbow sharply into Evan's stomach, and for a moment he dropped the reins and the horse slammed to a halt. Turning to look at her, he saw her nostrils flaring and recalled—too late—her fiery temper. It didn't show itself often, but when it did, it was a force to be reckoned with.

"How dare you try to force your will on me, Evan Campbell! I'm the one who stayed home and nursed Mama those long months after Papa died! While you abandoned us for a hedonistic life in London!"

Evan's head jerked back. Never before had she remonstrated with him regarding his irresponsible behavior following his father's death. Nor had Mama shown him anything but joy when he returned home like the prodigal son after running through his fortune and having nowhere else to go. Both had embraced him and showered him with love and forgiveness, and, after their mother's death, it was Ellen who had brought him back to his faith and whose inheritance supported the two of them in Oxford while he attended divinity school. He owed Ellen.

Ellen's hand covered her mouth. "Evan—I'm sorry! I never meant to say that. That was the past. Things are different now. *You* are different. Please forgive me!"

He placed an arm over her shoulders and drew her close. "There's nothing to forgive. I let you both down—and Papa too—and instead of the recriminations that I deserved, you repaid me with unfailing love and forgiveness. You have every right to remind me of it when it seems I've become a parsimonious prig."

Ellen reached for his right hand and clasped it in hers. "A parsimonious prig? You? Not likely! You're concerned for me, and you have a right to be." She swallowed. "I don't understand it, Evan, but something tells me this post was meant for me. I don't know why. If it's Lord Stanton—well—I have no intention of attaching some other woman's betrothed, but..."

She squeezed his hand and looked directly into his eyes. "My reasons for wanting to do this are *not* evil or immoral, Evan. I'm sure of it. I'm a grown woman, a spinster really. Please trust me."

Evan sighed. He had a pretty good idea of what was enticing her to Blackburn Court, and he was certain it would lead to heartache. But she was twenty-five and had a good head on her shoulders. She had a right to make her own decisions.

"If you insist, my dear. For a fortnight only. And I'll take you there and collect you every evening."

She squirmed in her seat. "Oh, well, that won't be necessary. Lord Stanton will send his father's coach for me."

Evan had a vision of Stanton and Ellen riding in a carriage alone by moonlight, and he felt his face redden. In the end, they agreed that Blackburn's carriage would collect her in the morning and that he himself would manage the return trip at the end of the day. That way, at least, he could determine when exactly *was* the end of the day.

More than three weeks later, Evan found himself more and more distracted with worry for his sister.

As much as she tried to hide it from him, when she returned to the vicarage each night, she was a different person. Distracted, alternately euphoric and morose, she eagerly awaited the earl's carriage every morning, finding reasons—excuses, really—for Lord Stanton to bring her home in the evening. Even after a permanent nurse had been employed, she persisted in arguing that she was still needed.

"Of course, I must help her get her bearings," she had explained, not meeting his eye. "Lord Blackburn prefers me to read to him over anyone else," was her excuse a few days later. And then she stopped making excuses at all, but simply shrugged when he mentioned it and went on with what she was doing.

That was when he feared the worst.

Whatever Ellen was doing at Blackburn had little to do with nursing. She was engaged in a flirtation—or more—with the earl's handsome heir who'd been betrothed to a duke's daughter since childhood.

And he didn't know what to do about it.

Chapter Two

1 December 1817
Huntingdon Manor
East Winch, Norfolk

"My dear girl, the entire county is wondering when you and young Stanton intend to tie the knot."

Lady Tilton, wife of the Viscount Tilton, had the dubious distinction of being the most meddlesome gossip of the area, possibly even the shire. As much as she was universally disliked, she was a long-time close friend of Queen Charlotte, and even the lofty patronesses of Almack's did not dare to cut her. As a prominent citizen of the King's Lynn society, she felt it her duty to oversee the affairs of gentility and bestow upon them the great gift of her wise counsels.

Alicia squirmed in her seat. Despite having sent a note over to Blackburn Court upon their arrival three days ago, she hadn't received a response from her betrothed, and she had no more idea of her wedding date than the rest of the county.

"Indeed," spoke up one of the ladies who seemed to gravitate around Lady Tilton. "He's been seen a great deal with that young lady who was supposed to be nursing his father. Quite pretty too."

"Scandalous," chided another of Lady Tilton's hangers-on "An unmarried lady nursing a gentleman? Unheard of! And why is she still there, after a more suitable nurse has been taken on? Unsavory doings, I don't doubt. That young man is a rapscallion if I ever saw one!"

Milton—a rapscallion? Alicia couldn't believe it. He might have kicked up a few traces in London in his earlier days, but here in Norfolk, with his father on his deathbed? Not likely.

"They say Miss Campbell nursed her parents for many years until their deaths," defended Mrs. Green, who was fond of contradicting Lady Tilton's pronouncements. "She is the perfectly respectable sister of the vicar of Castle Acre parish."

"Oh Eliza, you only say that because you wanted the young Mr. Campbell to notice your daughter Celia. How is that working out, by the way? Have they set a date for the wedding?" The sarcasm was palpable.

Mrs. Green flushed. "The vicar refused her offer of assistance due to a concern for her reputation. The blacksmith's wife has been doing for him. But Celia has sent over a few meals and he declares that she is a first-class cook." She preened as a good mother should.

"Well, I cannot imagine what he is thinking to allow his sister to be hanging out at Blackburn the way she is without any plausible justification for it. She and the viscount have been seen together everywhere, without any concern for propriety. My housekeeper's niece is a kitchen maid there and she says they ride together every day, for hours at a time! I'm sure if his father were up to snuff he'd put a stop to it, but the way things stand now, young Stanton does as he pleases."

Lady Tilton's lips flattened as she pronounced her judgment on the ramshackle Blackburn household.

"Well he *is* the next earl," Alicia pointed out. "And a fine one he'll be, when the time comes. He's always been so dutiful and responsible... I can't believe that will ever change."

Her loyalty to her betrothed notwithstanding, she *was* a bit disturbed by this nurse woman hovering around him. Not that she'd ever let on to *these* ladies, though. Perish the thought of her —a duke's daughter—being tossed aside for mere nobody.

Lady Tilton narrowed her gaze. "Are you not at least somewhat distressed that your intended has been seen about a great deal with another lady?" She shook her head. "My word! Betrothals have been known to be broken, you know. Not even the daughter of a duke is immune from the threat of having her betrothed's heart stolen by another."

Alicia forced a smile. "I do thank you for your concern, Lady Tilton, but I have every confidence in my fiancé's constancy. We've been the best of friends for the whole of our lives."

"No doubt the vicar's sister is lending him spiritual guidance," quipped one of the ladies, and they all tittered, except for Alicia and Mrs. Green.

Later, after the ladies had been sent off, Alicia's stepmother drew her back into the drawing room and closed the door.

"Alicia," she hissed, "you really must secure your connection to Stanton *immediately!* I assure you that the vicar's sister is *not* providing your betrothed with any spiritual advice. You've been foolish to neglect him these past years, and if you don't do something now, she'll have her hooks firmly entrenched and you will end a spinster!"

Alicia crossed her arms around her chest. "What nonsense, Elise! Are you so eager to be rid of me? Milton would never jilt me, but even if he did, there are other gentlemen, you know. Why do you assume that he is my only hope for marriage?"

She swallowed as she recalled that Milton had thus far uncharacteristically ignored her message. "I'm sure he's been preoccupied with the responsibility of running the estate and the distress of his father's illness."

"Mark my words," said her stepmother, flashing a cold smile, "you are going to lose Blackburn if you continue this blind trust that your childhood friend would never jilt you. Men's heads are ever turned by pretty faces, and only a fool would assume that any amount of affection would endure a prolonged separation."

Alicia pressed her lips together to keep herself from responding with the venom bursting to be released. Milton ensnared by a pretty face? Well, it did happen, of course. No doubt Elise knew how it was done, since she'd used hers to successfully ensnare a duke.

"I believe I shall visit my brother before Nurse puts him down for his nap," she said as she stalked out of the room, leaving Elise red-faced and furious. Refusing to engage in arguments was the best way she'd found to provoke her stepmother, who was constantly trying to prove her authority.

So Alicia did it often.

Later however, as she reached out to gather up little Gervase in her arms, she began to wonder if her betrothal was indeed jeopardized by the pretty vicar's sister. Perhaps she should pay the Gardiners a call and discover for herself what was going on at Blackburn Court.

She settled back in the rocking chair and cradled the six-month-old in her arms as she cooed over his squirmy, soft body. "I shan't be a spinster," she told him. "I shall have a brood of beautiful babies like you, sweeting, and make Elise a grandmother before she is thirty."

And with that thought, she settled him against her shoulder and rocked him to sleep, visualizing with pleasure the expression on Elise's face when someone addressed her as "Granny."

* * *

Later that day
Blackburn Court

The sun was already well on its way toward the western horizon by the time Evan reached the crossroad that would take him to Blackburn Court. Once he'd made his decision to confront Stanton about his intentions toward his sister, Evan had been impatient to make it happen. Determined to bring Ellen home with him—for good—he opted to take the cart, even though it was much slower than riding the horse would be. Already irked by Stanton's insistence on accompanying Ellen home from Blackburn Court in recent days, Evan was not about to allow him even one more minute alone with her.

I've got to be the strong one now. I'm the head of the family. I cannot allow my sister to be seduced by a predatory nobleman who will no doubt toss her aside for another when he's finished with her and leave her to her ruin.

As sixteen-year-old Mary Fuller in the Castle Acre cemetery had been (or so he imagined).

As usual, the doubts swarmed in his consciousness, reminding him of his past, that he was in no way qualified to judge his sister's actions. He'd indulged in much worse misdeeds, and not that long ago. The memories never failed to confound him when he sought to counsel a parishioner or prepare a sermon. He'd been out living a life of debauchery in London while his sister nursed their mother. Ellen was a *saint* compared to him! How did a sinner like him *dare* to offer spiritual advice to others!

But this time he pushed those thoughts away and instead began running through his mind the conversation he intended to have with Stanton. No doubt this man had charmed his way into Ellen's heart, overcoming her natural good sense. Someone needed to rein her in. Unfortunately, *he* was all she had. And he was determined that he would not fail her.

Perhaps he should ask to speak to Stanton alone, he thought, recalling his sister's defiance whenever he'd brought up the matter in the past. He'd even tried to catch the two of them together when Stanton's carriage pulled up to the door of the vicarage. But the most he'd seen—other than the exchange of heated looks as they made their farewells—was a slight pressing of the gloved hands together after he helped her alight from the carriage. Nothing he could find outwardly objectionable, really, unless one counted the powerful connection between them—an awareness of each other that went beyond the physical. In his lifetime he'd seen it in only a handful of couples—one being a friend of his who had fallen in love with his mistress, with disastrous results—and he could not envision this connection of his sister's ending well.

"What are your intentions regarding my sister?" seemed like a good way to begin. The man could hardly argue honorable intentions since he already had a fiancée. Of course, he might take offense and challenge him, but Evan didn't think he'd want the notoriety a duel would cause, and besides, Evan himself was handy with his fists. He'd trained with Jackson himself, and was a lapsed member of the Pugilistic Club.

Stanton didn't have a violent reputation. In fact, he didn't seem the type to deliberately ruin an innocent young lady. Perhaps there was some other reason for Ellen's presence at Blackburn Court. In the absence of a mistress in the household, perhaps she was assisting the housekeeper. Or cataloguing books in the library. Or...

Not a chance. She would have admitted it openly had that been the case. And he couldn't downplay the expression on her face whenever she mentioned the earl's son, and the way Stanton personally accompanied her on those daily carriage rides. He frowned. The evidence pointed to something nefarious going on, and he had to put a stop to it.

By the time he was approaching the winding, tree-lined drive leading to Blackburn Court, he had worked himself into an indignant rage. He urged the aged horse faster and almost missed seeing the injured female waving at him from the meadow about fifty yards from the road.

Reluctantly, he pulled old Ella to a halt, hopped out of the cart, and eyed the hedgerow for any gaps.

"There's a gate over there," the girl called, pointing to a corner about a furlong down the road he'd just traveled.

"Oh, I'm sure I can get over it," he insisted, putting a foot on a narrow branch and sliding his other leg over the top. Too late, he discovered there were brambles. So much for heroic gestures.

"There's a blackberry bush on this side," the girl offered. "They have the most dreadful thorns, you know. I should have warned you."

"Yes, well, I suppose I needed a new overcoat anyway." He couldn't see the extent of the damage, but he'd heard the distinct sound of a tear as he'd landed on the other side—on his feet, miraculously enough—and he wasn't about to mention that it could have been the crotch of his buckskin pantaloons.

"I shall be sure to replace it," the girl said with a toss of her dark brown hair. "Papa just gave me my pin money for the quarter, and goodness knows, there's nothing to spend it on here."

A genteel young lady, then. One with a father with deep pockets. Quite commonplace in London's exclusive drawing rooms, but not so much in King's Lynn. Stunning too, he realized as he made his way toward her. Wavy hair falling about her shoulders, she made an attractive picture sitting on the ground in her blue velvet riding habit.

"No need. Are you injured, then, madam?" He looked around in vain for a horse.

"My ankle," she said, wincing as she pointed to her left boot. "I think it's swollen because I can't get the boot off. Watch out for the marshy spots!" She warned him as he came to a clump of high grass. "I forgot the fens extended into Blackburn land. Merlin—that's my horse—stepped into one and unseated me when he pulled out his foot to escape."

"I see. And Merlin-er-bailed out on you?"

"Not at all," she said with a superior look. "Merlin is a highly-trained stallion, you know. I sent him home to fetch help. But it's much better that you have come along. It will be dark soon, and I wasn't sure how long it would take them to find me."

He caught a hint of fear in her golden-brown eyes before it was replaced with confident self-assurance.

"It would be my pleasure to escort you home, Miss—?" Then he realized she didn't know him either, so he added hurriedly, "Evan Campbell, at your service."

"Lady Alicia Howland, from Huntingdon Manor," she said with a bright smile on her imminently kissable lips. *Where had that thought come from?*

He bent down and examined the boot. "It will have to be cut off. I'm afraid I don't have a knife with me, however. I suppose the thing to do is to carry you to my cart"—he was suddenly embarrassed by his humble equipage— "and convey you to Blackburn Court where a doctor may be summoned."

She nodded hesitantly. "I suppose you are right. Huntingdon is only a mile from here as the crow flies, but this little mishap has caused me to recall that it's best to take the road than risk the fens this time of year."

As he bent down to gather her in his arms, she added, "I think you'd best use the gate this time. I hope I'm not too heavy."

"I'll manage," he said shortly. At six feet two and broad-shouldered, he was hardly a weakling. Was she afraid he would drop her?

She was no lightweight, though. Taller than average, with curves in all the right places, she was a pleasing armful rather than a burden. The feel of her arms around his neck and the proximity of her chest to his made his body stir with desires he hadn't felt since... well, not for a very long time. He thought he'd managed to drive out the old Evan, the dissolute young man with nothing to do but seek his own pleasure. But there were times when his nemesis came back to haunt him. Like now, when he held a beautiful woman in his arms.

"Where were you headed, Lady Alicia? A bit late in the afternoon for a young lady to be riding alone."

She sighed. "I-I started out later than I intended, and I didn't have time to wait for a groom. I was quite eager to see my fiancé, Lord Stanton, of Blackburn Court. I had something rather important to discuss with him, you see."

Evan felt a sudden coldness at his core. Fiancé? Lady Alicia belonged to another? The letdown he felt clouded his mind for a long moment before he made the connection.

Lady Alicia was Stanton's betrothed. Ellen's rival, so to speak.

* * *

Was that rumbling noise coming from her rescuer? Alicia's head swung around instinctively to scrutinize his face, which she had remarked earlier to be quite agreeable to look at. Almost as attractive as Milton, if you admired dark good looks. Which, she had to admit, most women—and she was no exception—did.

A slight frown disappeared almost immediately, followed by an unreadable expression. Perhaps she imagined it. Or perhaps Mr. Campbell had taken Milton in dislike for some reason? That was unlikely. Everyone liked Milton.

Mr. Campbell, on the other hand, was a stranger, albeit a well-dressed one. Even a highwayman could dress and behave like a gentleman. An unscrupulous man might easily take advantage of her situation and ruin her. Even being seen alone with him would provoke the sort of gossip that could taint her reputation, much less being seen *carried in his arms!*

"You must be new in King's Lynn, Mr. Campbell. I don't recall seeing you before."

"I am a rather recent arrival, but not in King's Lynn. I became the vicar in Castle Acre more than a year ago."

A vicar! Thank heavens! She turned her eyes heavenward for a brief second. A handsome young vicar was surely the best possible sort of rescuer. But then... the vicars she knew were either middle-aged or ancient and definitely not Sir Galahad types. She couldn't imagine any of *them* having the strength to carry her more than ten feet. Of course, it would be extremely inappropriate to feel any sort of attraction to one's rescuer either, but that information didn't seem to have reached her brain, because she was definitely feeling lightheaded and very feminine from the sense of being held in Mr. Campbell's strong arms.

Uh—that would be the *Reverend* Mr. Campbell, she realized with growing horror. Perfect for a rescuer, but definitely not an appropriate match for a duke's daughter. She took a deep breath and tried to control her physical reaction to him. But the thought did occur to her that she'd never felt such feelings for Milton Gardiner, nor any other man of her acquaintance. Of course, she'd never been carried in the arms of a man before, except perhaps her father when she was small. Perhaps this was why unmarried ladies and gentlemen were kept at discreet distances from each other and wore gloves in each other's company.

"You seem rather young to be a vicar, Mr. Campbell. I've met curates older than you are."

He had dimples when he smiled. And dark brown eyes that danced with humor.

"My congregation seems to agree with you. I can't tell you how many times I've been advised to marry and start a nursery as soon as possible in order to give myself more consequence. Although one long-married older gentleman suggested I grow a beard instead."

She smiled. "I suppose the mothers persist in throwing their marriageable daughters at you. Single young gentlemen are often difficult to find, particularly handsome ones with the means to support a family."

Oh dear. She probably should not have mentioned that she found him attractive. She really should not be flirting with him. Not just because he was beneath her, but because she was already betrothed.

He chuckled. "I *have* been introduced to an abundance of young ladies with superior housekeeping skills, at least according to their mothers. Fortunately, I have a sister living with me who manages my household quite well, so I am safe for the time being, at least."

A sister. A vicar with a sister heading for Blackburn Court. She closed her eyes. The sister whose presence at the Court was the reason for Alicia's sudden need to talk to her betrothed.

"Your sister is the nurse."

"Indeed," he said as he set her down in the weathered bed of the wagon, where he propped up her injuries foot on a wooden toolbox. "And you, I gather, are the fiancée."

They looked at each other for a long moment, and then he broke away and shrugged.

"I must apologize for the humble vehicle. My intention was only to convey my sister home from Blackburn Court. Had I known I would be rescuing a beautiful princess, I would have brought my golden carriage instead."

Alicia chuckled. "More a bedraggled, muddy wretch than a princess. But I do thank you for your gallantry."

"My pleasure, your ladyship." Doffing his hat, Mr. Campbell climbed up onto the bench and urged the horse forward.

For the few minutes it took to arrive at the entrance of Blackburn Court, Alicia stared at the pleasant sight of Mr. Campbell's back as she reflected on the situation with the Campbells and what—if any—significance they would have on her life and Milton's. The uncertainty of the future and the increasing pain of her ankle as the wheels of the rickety cart rotated over the cobblestone drive was beginning to make her head ache. Thank heavens they hadn't far to go. Mrs. Berry, the housekeeper, who had known her since she was a small tyke, would surely know what to do to make it all better.

"Bloody hell!"

The cart stopped abruptly and Alicia used her hands to pull herself into a sitting position, causing her ankle to drop painfully to the wagon bed. Biting her lips to keep from crying out, she peered past Mr. Campbell to see what had caused the young vicar to blaspheme in a most un-vicar-like manner.

It was Milton and some woman sitting in a curricle. And they were kissing. Passionately.

Alicia began to laugh hysterically. What else was there to do?

Chapter Three

"Unhand my sister, Stanton! Ellen, get over here. Now!"

The lovely sister's face turned fiery red as she realized her brother had witnessed their embrace.

Milton was on the ground in a flash. Had he been armed, Alicia mused in the throes of shock, he would surely have come at them brandishing a sword to protect his inamorata.

"Look here, Campbell, my intentions are honorable..." Then he recognized the person in the wagon bed and swallowed.

"Alicia... my dear."

"Milton! How *could* you?"

His inamorata? Dear God! The truth was beginning to sink in. Milton had indeed betrayed her.

"The gossip mill had it right," she said in disbelief. "The ladies told me I was a blind fool to trust you, Milton, but I couldn't accept it. I defended you! I actually *enjoyed* dismissing their accusations and boasting of your good character."

Milton crumpled under her scrutiny. "Alicia..."

If not for her injured ankle, Alicia would have stalked away and left him to stew until he was truly contrite and ready to grovel. Because she didn't think she'd ever forgive him otherwise.

Campbell was taking long strides toward the curricle and a glaring Milton forestalled him, reaching Ellen's side first.

"Allow me to help you, Ell—Miss Campbell," he said as he tenderly assisted her to the ground.

The pair exchanged brief whispers until he squeezed her hand and turned her in the direction of her brother. She took a few steps, then hesitated and turned to look back at Milton. He pursed his lips together and nodded reassuringly, and she made her way slowly and defiantly to the cart.

Mr. Campbell wheeled around and gave Alicia an impatient look, and she realized that he would have done and said much more had it not been for her injured presence. She herself had no desire to speak to Milton at the time, let alone spend five minutes with him, but the alternative—being conveyed to her home in the presence of the "other woman" was equally repugnant. In any case, her ankle pained her dreadfully, and she couldn't bear the thought of waiting until she returned to Huntingdon to get relief.

"If you would be so good as to see me inside, Mr. Campbell," she said with a glare at Milton, "I'm sure Mrs. Berry can tend to my ankle."

Mr. Campbell inclined his head toward her and began to lift her in his arms when Milton came running to her side.

"Alicia, you're hurt? I did not realize... Take your hands off her, Campbell! I'll take her inside! What did he do to you, my dear?"

Alicia rolled her eyes. "He did *nothing* to me, you-you *blackguard!* No, no, don't you dare touch me, Milton! Mr. Campbell was kind enough to rescue me when I tumbled from my horse just outside your gate and I trust him to help me inside. *You* I don't even wish to speak to at the moment."

Milton stopped in his tracks and gave a heavy sigh before turning to follow them into the house, his hands covering his face. Alicia turned away from him and noticed that Mrs. Berry and a handful of servants had already gathered at the door, indicating that the entire wretched scene must have been witnessed by the household staff.

"Oh dear, you've been injured, Lady Alicia? Jenkins, prepare the Green Room. Miller, fetch Nurse. I'm sure she can be of help since Lord Blackburn is napping at present."

Alicia let out a huge breath, relieved to be putting herself into Mrs. Berry's competent hands. She'd certainly patched up many scrapes and cuts over the years, between her and Milton... Oh dear, she didn't want to think about Milton at the moment.

"Thank you, Mrs. Berry. I would be grateful for the nurse's assistance—perhaps some ice to bring down the swelling—but I'm sure I am well enough to return home tonight. You need not prepare a room for me."

Mrs. Berry hesitated, finally indicating the drawing room. "You can put her in here for the present, Mr. Campbell. The chaise would be best, I suspect. Eames, fetch me some cushions for elevating that ankle."

Mr. Campbell placed her gently down on the settee indicated by the housekeeper, and looked at her apologetically.

"Are you sure you wish to remain here, Lady Alicia?" He glared at Milton, who was standing awkwardly in the doorway. "It would be my pleasure to convey you to your home."

Alicia flushed and smiled ruefully. "I assure you that I shall be well cared for here, Mr. Campbell. I've had the run of this house from infancy, after all. If you could but leave word at Huntingdon of my presence here on your way home, I should be exceedingly grateful. My horse, no doubt, has already returned without me and I shouldn't wish my father to launch a search party, especially as it is nearly dusk."

She felt a tingling warmth in her body as he bowed and kissed her gloved hand. "I do sincerely thank you for your kindness in retrieving me from the fens. I have to confess that I was quite concerned that night would come and my predicament not be relieved until morning."

"It was all my pleasure, ma'am," he said with a warm gleam in his eyes as he looked at her. "My best wishes for your quick recovery." He shook his head. "And I do apologize for the... unpleasant scene that followed. I know you must be exceedingly distressed, and I apologize for my sister's part in it."

To her surprise, Alicia didn't feel terribly distressed, and it worried her. Anyone else would have been furious at the sight of her betrothed's betrayal, but after the initial shock, all that concerned her most was the uncertainty of her future, now that she had no fiancé, or at least she assumed that was the case. Whatever *he* thought, she was in no way willing to saddle herself with a husband who cared for another woman.

"I'm sorry too," she replied. "But I do hope we shall meet again under more pleasant circumstances."

I should be heartbroken, she told herself. The young ladies in gothic novels felt like throwing themselves over cliffs when their lovers abandoned them. At the very least, they pined away into a decline. Alicia felt more like clubbing Milton over the head with a fireplace poker and leaving his dead body for the buzzards to pick on. Because now she would have to listen to Elise's crowing over her that she was right about Milton jilting her for another woman.

She let her head fall against the upholstery. "Ice," she said aloud. How long could it possibly take for someone to fetch ice from the ice house? Her ankle was throbbing painfully. She was relieved when Mrs. Berry returned with the nurse at her side.

Finally.

* * *

Evan's fists clenched as he approached the doorway where that blackguard Stanton hovered.

"Don't think this is over," he hissed. "You may believe yourself entitled to disport with the affections of any lady you choose, but when it concerns my sister, you are sadly mistaken!"

"But I'm not disporting with her—"

Evan was that close to planting his fist in Stanton's face when a white-faced Ellen inserted herself between them.

"Evan, don't! Let us go home and calm down, and discuss it later, like rational, God-fearing beings!"

Thus reminded of his vocation, Evan put his fist down reluctantly. Damn, if she didn't know how to get to his weak spot.

Seizing her by the arm, he pulled her with him toward the door, tossing back a warning to stay away from his sister.

"She's already the talk of the shire because of you! If you have any decency left, you'll leave her be and make peace with Lady Alicia for the wrong you've done her."

For a moment he thought Stanton was about to protest, but the mention of his betrothed seemed to take the wind out of the man's sails.

What a scoundrel to humiliate his betrothed in such a manner! A lovely, vibrant duke's daughter, an heiress to boot! He ought to thank his lucky stars for his good fortune instead of sniffing after innocent young ladies who couldn't help but be susceptible to his charm!

"It's not what you think," Ellen said when they had driven in silence for a few minutes. "Milton is not trifling with me. He's not like that."

"All men are like that."

"Not Milton. He loves me. We love *each other*."

Evan curled his lips. "*Lord Stanton* is a viscount, soon to be an earl. Far above your touch, even if he didn't already have a duke's daughter for a fiancée. Do you really expect him to make an honest woman of you? Or are you prepared to become his mistress?"

At that point many women would have slapped him, but not Ellen. She sat stoically at his side, her back straight and head held high. He glanced at her face and imagined he saw tears in her eyes in the darkness. That was Ellen. Always the controlled, unemotional type. The sort who could make you feel ashamed with one look at her disappointed eyes. The truth is, he'd never known her to waver in her faith, and he found it impossible to believe even now that she could have fallen so far.

He took one hand off the reins and used it to cover her tightly clasped hands. "I'm sorry, my dear. I don't really believe you would agree to such an arrangement. But your conduct has been so far out of the ordinary of late that I don't know what else to think but that Stanton has been leading you on."

She withdrew a hand and used it to swipe at her eyes.

"You don't know him, Evan! He's not like most—some men—who care for nothing but their own pleasures and not a whit for the consequences. I'm not saying he hasn't caroused a bit with his friends in London on occasion, but he's not like-like..."

"Me, you mean," Evan finished in a monotone voice. It always came back to the fact that he'd been merrily sampling the fleshpots of London while his sister remained behind caring for their invalid mother. Nevertheless, he *was* the one with firsthand experience of the workings of a rake's mind, while she was inclined to believe rather naively that most people were exactly as they appeared to be.

"Not at all, Evan." Her tone softened and she placed a gentle hand on his shoulder. "How much longer will you allow your guilt to eat away at your confidence? You are a good man, Evan, and so says the person who knows you best. When will you realize that for yourself and move on with your life?"

Evan's jaw clenched. "Have you heard *nothing* I've been saying up to this point, Ellen? You have no idea what sort of life I lived. I could have debauched dozens of virgins for all you know. At the very least, you know I abandoned you and frittered away my inheritance. I'll never forgive myself for that."

"You should," Ellen said, clasping his arm. "I've given you *my* pardon countless times, you know."

Evan forced a laugh. "That's just it. You have not lived it yourself, so you cannot possibly understand the sort of evil that can reside inside a man, temporarily disguised as goodness, until the deception is revealed, too late to escape the consequences."

Pulling back on the reins to stop the horse, he turned to face her in the darkness.

"Tell me, Ellen, what did the two of you *do* all that time you were together at Blackburn Court? Not in the beginning, when you were nursing the earl. What were you doing *after* the arrival of the new nurse? And before you attempt to regale me with a long list of innocuous tasks, I beg you to explain what possessed you to be kissing a gentleman betrothed to another."

Ellen crumpled under his scrutiny.

"I-We never meant to hurt anyone. Please believe that, Evan. I would never have tried to steal another woman's beloved, nor would I respect a man who could fall in and out of love so easily. But this betrothal was made when both parties were children, because their mothers were friends. And there is a clause in the contract that allows either to withdraw without penalty if they prefer not to go through with the marriage. Milton was planning to comply until he met me, and once he became aware of the depth of his feelings for me, he had to consider how to break the news to *her*." Her chin trembled. "We never meant for her to find out—the way she did."

Evan pressed his lips into a fine line. "A clause in the contract, eh?"

"I didn't have it from him," she said confidently. "Lord Blackburn told me himself."

* * *

For the next few hours, Alicia's attention was focused on finding relief for her injured ankle. The resident nurse shook her head when she saw it and packed it with ice to relieve the swelling. The willow bark tea supplied by the housekeeper eased her pain only slightly, but it all came back in full force when she was transferred upstairs to the Green Room in the arms of a burly footman who, at one point, swayed a little too close to the bannister, causing further injury to her ankle.

Gritting her teeth with pain, Alicia waved away the apologetic footman once she was settled in the soft canopy bed. The nurse clucked sympathetically as she propped the leg up on a pillow and re-applied the ice.

"Once the swelling's gone down, we can cut off the boot and take a look at the injury. If it's broken, the doctor will have to be called in. But more 'n likely it's just a bad sprain," she added at Alicia's sudden grimace.

A maid entered the room and curtsied toward Alicia. "Nurse, his lordship is awake and wants to know what all the fuss is about."

The older woman brightened. "Well, that's a blessing, isn't it? Lord Blackburn hasn't taken interest in much of anything for days now. I'd better check on him. It's time for his medicine. Who knows? I might persuade him to take a bit of dinner."

Milton, who had apparently been hovering in the hallway, peeked in through the doorway.

"I'll sit with Lady Alicia until you return."

Nurse looked skeptical. "I don't think..."

Alicia frowned. "Go away, Milton. I can't talk to you now."

"But Alicia... We've always been close. It agonizes me to think that I have caused you pain."

Alicia closed her eyes and opened them again. "You didn't cause me to fall off my horse," she said tiredly. "As for the rest... perhaps you deserve to suffer for a time."

"As you wish," he said sadly. "I wish you well, my dear." And then he was gone.

Dull eyes, slumped shoulders, heavy-footed—poor Milton was truly suffering. He wasn't the sort to wallow in misery. She couldn't recall seeing him so since-since... the boating accident. The one in which they'd lost both their mothers. One could hardly expect otherwise under the circumstances.

But why should she feel sorry for him now? He'd brought all this on himself. Oh, she'd probably forgive him in the end. How could she do otherwise? But he'd made her a laughingstock. And

Miss Campbell too, come to that. Even worse, *she* was probably ruined. And her charming brother, a vicar, would be tarnished as well. Such a shame. It was really too, too bad of Milton to dally with a proper young lady.

The remainder of the evening was a blur after her father and Elise arrived, the doctor in tow, and she was given a dose of laudanum to alleviate the pain as the doctor cut off her boot and examined her bruised ankle. She vaguely recalled hearing that the foot was not broken, that the sprain would heal in a few weeks if she would keep off it, and that she could be moved home in a day or two if the swelling stayed down.

She also recalled Elise bending down and congratulating her on the brilliance of her scheme to secure her betrothal. Scheme? Her stepmother thought her fall from the horse was intentional? She'd wanted to protest, but her mind was too fuzzy and all she wanted to do was close her eyes and forget.

Chapter Four

*The next evening
Blackburn Court*

"Pardon me, my lady, but his lordship would like to speak with you, if you are feeling better."

Alicia, who was seated at the desk, her leg propped up on a chair and a green velvet pillow, writing to a friend in London, hesitated only a moment to glance at the speaker and shake her head before returning to her correspondence.

"Tell the viscount I'm occupied," she told the nurse. She wanted Milton to suffer a bit longer before she would forgive him.

"Begging your pardon, my lady, but it's not Lord Stanton. It's the earl himself who requests to speak with you."

Alicia dropped her pen. "Lord Blackburn?" She was eager to talk once more with the man who'd been like an uncle to her all her life, but she'd been told that he wasn't up to it.

"His health is improved, then? I am delighted to hear it!" She lowered her injured leg to the floor and made a tentative effort to stand.

"Oh no! The doctor said you're not to stand on it, ma'am. No indeed. We have brought you his lordship's Bath chair."

"Oh, but surely that won't be necessary..." she began, recalling the three-wheeled, wicker contraptions and their elderly occupants from Bath and other watering holes she'd visited. She halted when she saw Milton propelling the chair into her room.

"Good evening, Alicia. How are you this fine evening? I understand your ankle is much improved."

"Much better, thank you, my lord," she said with a frown. "I understand your father is asking for me. Does that mean...?"

Milton shook his head sadly. "His consciousness goes in and out, but his prognosis has not changed. If he lasts much past the New Year, the doctor would be much surprised." He swallowed. "Nevertheless, I relish the times we have together during his periods of lucidity. He is much the same man he always was, despite his frail appearance."

There was a brief silence, and then Milton spoke.

"If this creaky contraption does not please you, Alicia, I would be delighted to carry you myself, of course."

The comic expression on his face had her struggling not to laugh. It was difficult to be angry with Milton. He'd always been able to charm his way out of anyone's bad humors.

"The chair is fine. Nurse, if you could just assist me a bit..."

Milton held the chair steady as Alicia hobbled into the seat with the nurse's help.

"That's it," the older lady said as she tucked a lap robe over Alicia's legs. "Won't do to catch a chill from the drafts in the hall. His lordship's got a blazing fire, so you'll be comfortable there."

Milton dismissed the nurse and carefully guided the chair into the hallway.

"We *must* speak, Alicia, and soon. I understand you are returning to Huntingdon in the morning."

"I know," she replied, feeling a pang of guilt for making him suffer. Of course she would forgive him. How could she not? They'd always been the best of friends. But if he wished to continue the betrothal... she couldn't work up any enthusiasm for wedding a man she couldn't trust.

For a moment Evan Campbell's face flashed in her mind, but she dismissed it as a temporary attraction. The trauma of the accident combined with the pain of her ankle and the timely appearance of a handsome young rescuer... wouldn't any woman have been vulnerable at such a time?

"Perhaps after your conversation with Father," he whispered as he wheeled her into the master chambers.

She nodded silently and turned her attention to the withered man in the bed. Oh, how he had aged! She recalled the earl as a younger gentleman pushing her higher and higher in the swing under the old oak tree in the wood near where the tenants lived. Pulling her up in front of him on his horse while Milton trotted along next to them on his pony as they inspected the fields. The time when he sat them both down on a bench in the stable and reprimanded them thoroughly for evading the nursemaid who was supposed to watch them and Alicia had nearly drowned while they were hunting frogs in the lake. It was heartbreaking to see him looking so debilitated.

Milton maneuvered the chair alongside the bed and ducked out of the room.

Alicia leaned over and clasped the earl's hand.

"It's good to see you again, my lord."

He smiled and slowly raised her hand to kiss it..

"My thought exactly, Alicia, my dear. I always knew you'd grow up to be a beauty. My Catherine loved you like a daughter, you know. She always wanted a little girl to spoil, but it never happened."

Alicia's eyes prickled with tears. "Mama always wanted a son like Milton too," she added.

The earl closed his eyes briefly and shook his head.

"They were so close, Catherine and Frances. It was their fervent wish to see their children wed and thus be connected forever through their descendants."

"I know," said Alicia, swiping at her wet eyes.

"There are handkerchiefs in that drawer next to you," he said helpfully.

"Thank you, my lord," she said as she obtained one from the drawer and dabbed at her eyes.

"We saw how you and Milton took to one another so quickly and became such good friends and it just seemed as though a marriage between you would be the best of all options. Joining estates would mean inheritances for two of your sons, not just the elder. The four of us would share grandchildren. And we would all live long and happy lives knowing that our descendants would be well-situated."

Alicia's vision blurred. If only her mother and Lady Blackburn had not taken the boat out that day...

The earl swiped at his own eyes. "They were so alive and vibrant... how could we have known their lives would be taken away so quickly? Very little of the life we planned has come to fruition. At first I thought it a cruel joke, and then—much later—I began to accept it as a lesson from the Almighty. We make choices in our lives, but in the end, we must learn to deal the best we can with what the Almighty sends our way."

He squeezed her hand weakly, and she was reminded of his frail health.

"Please do not tax yourself on my behalf, Lord Blackburn. Nurse—that is—all of us are concerned for your health."

The old man gave her a sad smile. "They all warn me not to waste my strength, but that's nonsense. The end will come when it comes and no sooner. And while I still live and breathe, I have things to say. To you especially, dear Alicia."

She blinked away tears at the thought of the earl's passing. "Then please do speak, your lordship. I will forever treasure your words in my heart."

"You and my son—the betrothal. It wasn't meant as an edict. We—your parents and Catherine and I—were eager—too eager, I suppose—to make the arrangements and work out the details of the marriage in the hope that the two of you—well, to facilitate your joining, if that was what you wished.

"However, our first concern was your happiness. While ours were love matches, we had all seen the tragic consequences of many arranged marriages in our set. We did not wish that for you and Milton. The betrothal was more of a suggestion, I suppose." He sighed and shook his head slowly. "A fantasy, really. It gave us pleasure to imagine our families united for all eternity."

Although his eyes were still directed at Alicia, she could see that what he was seeing was the dreams of the past. At one point she thought he had fallen asleep, but a moment later he shook himself out of it and continued as though he'd never stopped.

"So we were careful to include a clause that would clearly give either of you the right to withdraw from the betrothal without penalty should you decide to pursue another match."

Alicia blew out a puff of air. "That makes sense, I suppose. Child betrothals aren't really binding any longer, are they?"

The earl began coughing, and the nurse rushed in to give him some medicine.

"A few more minutes, no more," she warned Alicia, when the coughing at last came to a halt.

"Did Milton know he wasn't legally bound to me?" she demanded after the nurse had gone. If she'd known Milton could fall in love with someone else, she might have paid more attention to her beaux in London, looking for true love as her friends were. But Milton was her future—or so she'd thought—and her best friend seemed like the perfect choice for a husband, so she'd accepted it. But now—she recalled Milton and Ellen Campbell's kiss from the day before and began to understand where this conversation was going.

The earl shook his head. "I'm sure your mother would have told you, at the very least prior to your coming out, but she died too soon. Your father and I thought it best not to mention it for a while, since you were both—we were all of us—in mourning for our great losses, and then—I suppose we liked the idea so much ourselves, and there seemed to be no great attachment elsewhere for either of you—we decided to simply allow it to stand."

"Until now." Alicia brought a shaky hand to her forehead. "Milton wishes to marry the vicar's sister."

Milton was not the sort to dally with a respectable young lady. He must be serious about her after all.

A pained expression came over his face.

"I'm sorry, my dear. I would have loved to have you as my daughter in truth, but my son's heart has been taken by another, and... I sense that your feelings for him are—of a different sort, are they not?"

Once again the image of the handsome vicar popped into her head. Was it possible? She pushed it away, unable to see herself as a vicar's wife.

"I suppose so," she said doubtfully. She loved Milton. She always had. But they weren't... romantic feelings. She couldn't imagine kissing him as Ellen Campbell had.

"Time for his lordship to rest." The nurse burst in carrying a thick wool blanket.

"Talk to him," advised the earl. "He knows you're due an explanation, and he's been eager to set things straight with the two of you."

"Yes, my lord. Good night, sir."

Milton appeared out of nowhere—had he been eavesdropping?—and wheeled her out of the room.

"Shall we adjourn to the library? If you will allow me to carry you downstairs, Alicia?"

"Yes, I think that would be best." It wasn't a game any longer. This was real life. As much as she still had good reason to be angry with Milton, she realized she wasn't. Not really. If he had found his true love, she had to be happy for him. Except that it left her out in the cold, didn't it?

What a ridiculous thing to worry about! A duke's daughter could easily find a husband. One more suitable than a country vicar, of course.

Where did *that* thought come from?

* * *

The candles within their glass globes were well worn down by the time Milton arrived in the first-floor library with Alicia in his arms. That and the empty decanter of whisky on his father's desk indicated that Milton had spent some time brooding here before coming upstairs to check on her and his father. He appeared tired and avoided meeting her eyes as he set her down gently on a plush wing chair and brought a stool and pillow for her injured foot.

At that moment, Alicia's anger began to melt away and be replaced with compassion for her friend. His father was dying, and he would soon inherit the earldom and all that went with it. A role he'd been preparing for all his life, but she knew he wouldn't have chosen it for himself had he the choice. How he had chafed at not being allowed to purchase a commission and fight Napoleon's troops as his friends had! But his older brother had been stillborn and there were no children born after him. It was as the earl had said: there are choices to be made, but in the end, you must deal with life the best you can.

"Did you know??" she asked abruptly after Milton had drawn up a chair next to her. "That our betrothal wasn't meant to be binding?"

"I did," he said, staring down at his feet. "Father mentioned it before I left for my first Season in London. He said if I met someone I preferred over you, I should not believe myself tied—legally, of course—to the betrothal because it wasn't meant to be that way."

He raised his eyes to hers and she saw the remorse in them. "I never looked for anyone else, Alicia. I fully expected to marry you eventually and settle down here at Blackburn Court with our children. For a long while, I couldn't imagine marrying anyone else. And I believe you felt the same, didn't you? Beyond a bit of flirting and such, you didn't seem serious about any of the other gentlemen."

He pulled at his collar. "So when I first met Ellen, I was blindsided. I knew right away that she was my other half, and she did as well. I didn't know what to do. It wasn't supposed to happen. I'd never felt that way about any other woman—not any of the dozens of debutantes whose mothers threw them at me for all the four years I spent doing the social thing." He rolled his eyes. "In spite of the betrothal that was common knowledge. Apparently landing an earl's heir is worth a bit of scandal in the beginning. But I never met anyone I liked as well as you, Alicia."

"Until you met Miss Campbell."

He swallowed and looked longingly at the empty glass on the desk. "Can I get you something to drink, Alicia? Some wine or... something stronger, perhaps?"

She grinned. "It appears you've already drained the bottle."

He smiled self-consciously. "A subtle hint. Perhaps I *have* had enough. But I can send for another if you wish."

"None for me," she said, feeling relieved at the return to normalcy in their manner. "I've been dosed with medicines the whole day long. Quite frankly, I'm surprised I can still sit upright and converse in any meaningful way."

She leaned forward and patted his knee.

"Rest easy, my friend. I'm done with making you suffer. It was cruel of me to let you think that my heart was broken at your defection. I love you—and always will love you—as a cherished friend. I'm happy that you have found the love of your life, and I would never want you to renounce that to keep from disappointing *me*."

She sighed. "I must admit being wildly envious of your good fortune, though. I've never met anyone who made my heart flutter"—she tried to ignore the image of Evan Campbell that came to mind—"and I'm not sure I ever will."

Milton closed his eyes briefly and let out a huge breath. "You are far kinder to me than I deserve," he said finally. "I should have told you much sooner. You were owed *that* consideration at the very least. But it happened so quickly—our first meeting was only six weeks ago, you know—and I was reluctant to disappoint you and our fathers, although I knew it would have to be done at some point."

He flushed. "When you and Campbell saw us yesterday, Ellen and I had just agreed that I should go to you and confess all... and ask to be released from our commitment. We—weren't at all certain how you would react, Alicia, and there was at least a bit of fear that you would be angry or hurt and refuse... and I suppose we lost our heads for a moment."

Alicia hid a grin. So she was supposed to believe that was the first and only time the pair had embraced? But she decided to let it pass. They were truly in love and expected that she would react to the news with hysterics and recriminations. Which she had done, in a matter of speaking. Making him suffer a full day before deciding to forgive him. So cruel and unnecessary. Sometimes she didn't like herself very much.

"Please forgive me, Milton. I own it was quite a shock to see for myself that the rumors are true"—he paled at that—"but rest assured that my heart remains whole and unbroken, and now that I've had time to consider the matter, I am very happy that you and Miss Campbell found each other."

"You are too kind—" he began.

"Not at all," she said with a shake of her head. "I can be selfish and unkind and even vindictive on occasion. I'm sure if Mama were here, she'd give me a good scolding for some of the uncharitable things I have said."

Her shoulders quaked and Milton leaned forward to clasp her hands in his.

"Do not chastise yourself too severely, my dear. I know you as well as anyone does, and I know you have an inner spirit that is generous and loving."

Alicia wasn't so sure about that. Perhaps Milton had not heard about the scolding Lady Cowper had given her after overhearing her maliciously counsel Rebecca MacPherson to ease up on the bonbons before she split the seams in her bodice. Papa had *not* been pleased to hear about that when Elise reported it back to him.

And speaking of Elise... Alicia felt suddenly ashamed of the manner in which she taunted and teased her stepmother. Granted, their personalities were too different for them to ever be good friends, but civility between them should at least be possible.

Generous spirit? She'd seen few signs of it in recent years. Milton was well rid of her.

"You are an extraordinary man," she said with a sincere smile. "Your Ellen is a most fortunate woman. When do you plan to marry?"

Evan frowned and pushed the hair out of his face.

"We have discussed it," he confessed, "but we could not fix a date until you and I had spoken. It should be soon, while Father"—he took a deep breath—"can be present to witness it."

Alicia clapped her hands. "A Christmas wedding! There is still time enough to call the bans if you speak to the vicar directly."

Milton bit his lip. "That would be the Reverend Evan Campbell, Ellen's brother. He's been filling in for our own vicar, who is on leave." Alicia tittered with laughter. "And after what happened yesterday, I've been half-expecting him to challenge me to a duel rather than give me his blessing to wed his sister."

Chapter Five

5 December 1817
Huntingdon Manor

Huntingdon Manor was an impressive sight, especially with dark clouds hovering overhead signaling the onslaught of rain—or possibly even snow, Evan mused as he shivered in the cold carriage. His sister and Stanton, seated scandalously close together on the seat opposite, did not appear to notice the weather. Or the stately home. Or him, even. They were completely engrossed in each other, all smiles and heated glances as they clasped their gloved hands together.

Turning his attention back to the ducal manor, he thought he had never seen a home so magnificent. The expansive Palladian design was reminiscent of Devonshire House on Piccadilly Street, but as striking as that extravagant home appeared, the ducal seat of the Huntingdons was even more so, with its massive stone portico consisting of tall white Corinthian columns topped by an intricately-sculptured, triangular pediment between rows and rows of windows surrounded by an expanse of natural beauty that eclipsed any of the fine houses in London, even in winter.

The Duke of Huntingdon was a very important man indeed,

he reflected, to own such a home. With all the family wealth and exalted connections, no doubt Lady Alicia would make a splendid marriage once it was known her betrothal had been dissolved. She was well above *his* touch, of course. He grimaced. Where had *that* thought come from? He wasn't in the market for a wife.

The earl's coach came to a stop, and the two lovebirds suddenly seemed to become aware of their surroundings. When the coachman pulled down the steps, Stanton scrambled down and held out his hand for his betrothed. Evan winced. In spite of giving his reluctant assent to Stanton's request for his sister's hand in marriage, he still harbored doubts regarding the man's character. Considering that the so-called "courtship" was conducted in a rather ramshackle manner while Stanton was still betrothed to another woman, he worried about his sister's future happiness. Stanton's apology seemed sincere, however, and Ellen was generally a reliable judge of character, but as a genteel young woman, she couldn't know a great deal of the darker side of a man's nature. She had, after all, forgiven *him* far too easily for his own transgressions, and quite possibly she was making the same mistake with Stanton.

A butler and two footmen in elegant blue livery with gold trim took their wraps and showed them to a large drawing room with a roaring fire, where they were seated and informed that tea would be forthcoming.

The Duke of Huntingdon arrived soon after to greet them and be introduced to the Campbells. Evan was pleased to see no sign of antipathy on the duke's part as regards the rupture of his daughter's betrothal. On the contrary, he seemed quite sincere in his congratulations to Stanton and Ellen and even offered them the use of the Huntingdon ballroom for the wedding breakfast.

"Huntingdon dearest, what are you about making such offers without a word to me first?" All eyes turned toward a petite beauty with pale blond hair and cold gray eyes dressed in a green velvet gown trimmed in gold, which he thought more appropriate to a ball than an informal encounter such as this one.

"My wife, the duchess," said the duke, turning to greet his wife and present her to their guests. "The viscount, of course, is a close family friend," he said, with a slight emphasis on the *close family friend* part. "And this is his lovely fiancée, Miss Campbell, and her brother, Mr. Campbell. The vicar at Castle Acre parish, you know."

Evan, who, with the others, had risen upon the duchess's entry, bowed over her hand.

"A pleasure to meet you, your grace."

"Charmed," she said icily as she withdrew her hand, nodding curtly at Ellen's short bow.

"Delighted to see you again, your grace," Stanton said in his turn. "Rest assured that Ellen and I would not dream of imposing on you for the wedding breakfast. The ballroom at Blackburn, although not as handsome as yours, will do nicely for the occasion. Of course we hope my father will be well enough to attend some of the festivities, and he is not able to travel."

"We do not plan an elaborate affair, your graces," added Ellen, following his lead. "It will be a Christmas wedding and there isn't a great deal of time to make the arrangements." She gave a worried frown. "I have no experience planning such an affair, although I suppose Mrs. Berry will advise me."

"I'd love to help you, if you would allow me, Miss Campbell," said Alicia limping into the room on the arm of a footman.

Evan hurried to escort her to a settee next to him. She looked lovely in a cherry-striped day dress, her dark hair piled high and adorned with a pink bandeau. He could hardly take his eyes off her.

Mouths dropped as the other occupants of the room stared at her in surprise.

The duke was the first to recover. "Why Alicia, my dear, what an excellent idea! It will scotch all rumors of ill-feeling between you and Stanton."

"That is very generous of you," Evan started to say, but was cut short by the duchess, whose lips curled as she glared at her stepdaughter.

"How ridiculous! Alicia has no experience organizing social events. It will end a dreadful disaster and people will say she did it deliberately in revenge for having been jilted."

Alicia flushed and Evan wanted to speak out against her stepmother's deliberate insult, but his sister beat him to it.

"For my part, I would be delighted to accept Lady Alicia's offer." Ellen moved to Alicia's side, took her hand and squeezed it. "The two of us together, with Mrs. Berry's and Cook's assistance, can surely manage to put together a relatively small wedding breakfast. No doubt she knows far more than I, and besides, it will offer us the opportunity of becoming more closely acquainted. I know you are one of Evan's closest friends, my lady, and I hope your friendship will soon be expanded to include me." This last was offered to Alicia directly, who smiled warmly at her.

"Of course. You must call me Alicia, then."

"And I am Ellen."

The duchess made some excuse and stalked out of the room just as the tea trolley was ushered in. The duke invited Stanton into his study to discuss the legal matters associated with the termination of the betrothal, and Evan and the two ladies settled down to tea and conversation.

* * *

Alicia wasn't sure what had prompted her to volunteer to assist with Milton and Ellen's wedding. Ellen, after all, was the "other woman" only two days past. But she *was* Milton's love and now that she had forgiven him and they had returned to their old familiarity, she sincerely wished to see him happy. Ellen was beginning to grow on her too, particularly after she had so effectively countered Elise's set-down.

"Would you be so kind as to pour the tea, Miss-er-Ellen? As you can see, I am still a bit impaired."

"Of course."

Many young women would be intimidated serving tea in a ducal household, especially under these circumstances, but it didn't seem to faze Ellen. Alicia was impressed with the grace and poise with which she served them each with tea and crumpets.

"How is your ankle doing, Lady Alicia?" inquired Mr. Campbell once his sister had settled down with her own refreshments.

"Much better, although the doctor says I am not to walk on it for another week." She set her cup down on the table next to her. "But you must call me Alicia, as your sister does. I do hope we will all become friends. The country can be a dreadful bore in winter, once the holidays have passed." She clapped her hands in excitement. "But now we have a wedding to plan! A Christmas wedding too! How perfectly marvelous!"

"Allow me to thank you again for your offer of help, Alicia. I have hosted ladies' teas and sewing circles and such for the parish, but nothing quite so formal as a wedding breakfast. My own wedding breakfast." She swallowed. "I suggested to Stanton that we keep it small, but he says the entire neighborhood must be invited, as well as his close friends from other parts of England. Of course, they might not be able to come," she added hopefully. "Most people like to spend Christmas with their families."

"Milton is correct," affirmed Alicia. "A Blackburn wedding is a much-anticipated event. The tenants—both yours and ours—will wish to attend the breakfast, along with the villagers from as far away as Middleton and Narborough."

"Swaffham and Castle Acre as well," put in Mr. Campbell. "Our parishioners will wish to show their support, Ellen."

Ellen's hand shook and she quickly set her teacup down. "Oh dear. How shall we ever cope? I fear I shall turn out to be a most unsatisfactory viscountess!"

"Nonsense! Milton has every confidence in you, my dear. Besides, you have me to assist you. And Mrs. Berry and the Blackburn staff, and I daresay Papa will lend you our staff as well. It will be a grand adventure, just wait and see!"

Alicia was surprised to find herself genuinely excited at the prospect. While country society could never rival the thrill of London, there was something quite satisfying about helping make someone else's special day a success.

Ellen nodded, her eyes glowing. "How would I ever do it without you, dear Alicia! Milton and I will be in your debt."

"Make my good friend happy and that will be thanks enough," Alicia said with a smile. "Even better if it gets me out of the house and away from my stepmother for a while. We rather grate on each other," she added, a pinched expression on her face.

"Your father seems to handle it well," Evan offered after a poignant pause.

Alicia grinned. "Indeed, Papa is ever the duke in public. I'm sure there will be a bit of a brush-up between them later, however. In private. But then, he is already in Elise's bad books for not holding Milton to our betrothal." She grimaced. "I rather pity him having to mediate so often between the two of us. While the betrothal existed, Elise was hopeful that I would be removing from this house in short order. Since it appears I shall remain a thorn in her side for the foreseeable future, she is understandably disappointed."

"Has it always been so contentious between you?" Evan inquired. "Or did something happen to cause her to take you in dislike?"

Alicia sighed and shook her head. "On her part, I can't say for sure. In retrospect, however, I can say that I was predisposed to dislike her. I couldn't wish for Papa to replace Mama *ever*, but particularly not with someone half his age. She was so enchanted with the consequence due her as a duchess that I questioned her motives for wedding him." She bit her lip. "In retrospect I comprehend that it was between the two of them and not for me to conjecture, but that was also a bone of contention. Papa and I have been together for twenty-one years, and I didn't want an interloper coming between us."

"Perhaps in time you will learn to get on better," suggested Evan, with an encouraging smile.

"I hope so, for my father's sake," Alicia agreed. "And my brother's as well, of course. I am uncommonly fond of Gervase, despite Elise being his mother. He is the light of my life. Perhaps later we could visit the nursery so that you could make his acquaintance?" She directed a questioning look at Evan. "If you wish it, of course. I know some gentlemen find children bothersome."

"Not I," Evan denied. "I should love to make the young marquess's acquaintance."

"By all means," Ellen chimed in. "Stanton and I look forward to having children of our own, and we shall expect my brother to be a doting uncle."

They exchanged an amused look. Alicia envied their close relationship. As her parents' only child, she'd often wished for a handful of siblings. There was always Milton, of course. But with the onset of adulthood and his increased responsibilities, he hadn't been around much and she'd felt his absence keenly while in the country. Perhaps a friendship with his wife might ease that loneliness.

"You mean take him fishing and teaching him cricket? I could do that." Evan grinned.

"And if it's a girl?" Ellen teased.

Evan shrugged. "I'll take 'em all." He cocked his head. "As I recall, you were a fine cricketer. Or is that cricketress? Remember that fine trout you caught on Langmere Lake? It must have weighed close to ten pounds. Papa was so proud."

"I've always been a better fisherman than you," Ellen boasted. "Do you fish, Alicia? There must be some fine fishing sites around here."

"Oh yes. Mama was obsessed with sailing and fishing and she took me with her often." She sighed heavily. "The Wash was her favorite place, but the currents are strong and it can be quite dangerous. That is how she died, you know. And Lady Blackburn too. A sudden storm came up and they were tossed overboard. The local fishermen found them. It makes me shiver just to think about the Wash, let alone sail on it after that."

She stared briefly into the fire, and then perked up. "A wedding dress! A future countess must have a fine one, you know. I know an exclusive Bond Street modiste who will make one up for you in a fortnight, if the order is placed forthwith. My father will lend us his carriage. Shall we leave tomorrow morning, Ellen?"

Ellen gasped. "Oh dear, I shan't need a gown as grand as all that. Surely there are modistes nearby... in King's Lynn, perhaps."

The two engaged in a good-natured argument, and Alicia laughingly conceded that one of the local modistes would do a creditable job. By the time the ladies had made plans for a shopping trip on Monday, Milton and the duke had returned from their tête-à-tête, and from their affable manner, Alicia assumed that all was well between them. She watched Milton hasten to Ellen's side, kiss her hand, and bend over to whisper something in her ear that made her blush. There was something quite satisfying to witness their happiness, and Alicia felt more than a little envious. Would she ever find such a match for herself?

"Alicia, my dear, will you not show Mr. Campbell the portrait gallery while he is here? I have some matters to attend to in my study, and I'm sure the bridal couple have things to discuss."

He winked at her, and Alicia was quick to turn to Evan and repeat the offer. Evan accepted heartily and the three of them excused themselves and left the lovers alone.

"I shouldn't leave them alone too long," her father said softly as they cleared the threshold. "Propriety can be stretched slightly for an engaged couple, don't you agree, Mr. Campbell?"

"I do indeed, sir," Evan replied with a grin. "But only a minute or two. Certainly no longer than a quarter hour."

The duke grinned. "I'll keep m'door open and listen for anything untoward. The same warning goes for m'daughter too, especially as you are not bespoken. But I reckon a man of God can be trusted." He winked at Evan.

"Oh, Papa!" Alicia blushed. But she *had* noticed Evan sending admiring looks in her direction. Then she reproached herself for being silly. No one with any sense would imagine *her* to be seriously interested in a vicar. And surely a man of God would be looking for a woman who was pious, hardworking and selfless. A spoiled, selfish duke's daughter would never do.

* * *

Evan did his best to concentrate on Alicia's amusing commentary as she pointed out the somber-looking relatives portrayed in her family portraits. But it was increasingly difficult to do when he could feel her delightful curves as she leaned on his arm for support. His body was painfully aware of her as they made their way rather inelegantly around the room. But then, he would be attracted to any lady as lovely and charming as Alicia, would he not? It's just that he wasn't normally allowed to be in such close proximity to one. That had to be the reason, he told himself.

"Do you see the portrait of that lady carrying a Pekinese in her arms? That is my father's mother. She may have a sedate smile on her lips here, but Papa said she was always landing in scrapes. She was the daughter of a missionary to China, but you'd never know it by her behavior. She met my grandfather when she slipped away and attended a mill while dressed in her brother's clothing."

Evan raised his eyebrows and she laughed. "It was a bet, you see. She was always making wagers. Not for money or anything. She just enjoyed thumbing her nose at society. Grandpapa saw through her disguise immediately and said it was love at first sight."

Evan chuckled. "She must have been a most extraordinary duchess."

Alicia giggled and flashed her tawny eyes at him. He could swear he saw gold sparks emanating from them.

"Indeed. Her mother-in-law—my great-grandmother—demanded that her husband forbid the marriage, but he told her if she wanted grandchildren she'd have to learn to accept their mother along with them."

"A wise man, then."

"I believe he was. I imagine my father is much like him."

"And your mother? What was she like? If it does not pain you to speak of her, that is."

"Over there." She indicated a portrait on the adjacent wall, and he helped her hobble toward a painting of the duke as a young man and a smiling dark-haired woman.

"This was painted soon after their wedding. Sir Joshua Reynolds. Mama said he was very cross because she wouldn't keep still enough. But he managed to capture them both quite well, I believe," she said proudly. "But my favorite is the one of Mama in the green drawing room. It was painted a few months after my birth. She'd lost two babes before that, and they were both so delighted to have a child at last."

At the tremor in her voice, Evan looked down at her face and saw tears gathering.

"You grieve her still," he observed, "even after so many years." He handed her a handkerchief.

"Thank you. You are so kind. Well, yes, I suppose I shall always miss her. Even more, I wonder if my character might have been improved had she been around to counsel me."

Evan's eyes widened. "Why—?"

She shook her head. "Please allow me to finish, Mr. Campbell. I know I've been indulged and my ungenerous behavior tolerated due to my father's wealth and my status as a duke's daughter. Had I been anyone else, I'm sure I should never have received another voucher for Almack's after three of the patronesses heard me saying unkind things about His Grace the Duke of Wellington and his *chères-amies.*"

Evan raised his eyebrows. Most assuredly the duke's unhappy marriage and subsequent forays into the demimonde were commonly whispered about among the ton; however, such behavior was not condoned in a young, unmarried lady. So much the worse to be overheard by one of the highest sticklers of society!

"Mama was one of the kindest ladies in the ton," Alicia continued. "One of the premier political hostesses in London. She would have packed me off to the country for the rest of the Season if she'd been around to hear of it. As it was, Papa was in Scotland on his honeymoon, and my aunt who was sponsoring me scolded me and advised me to lie low until some other scandal occurred."

She shrugged. "She was right. By the next season, it was as though nothing had happened, and my stepmother was too ill with her confinement to come to London then, so she never found out." She shook her head. "Goodness knows she would never have let me forget it if she had!"

Evan cleared his throat. "I would hardly characterize the members of the ton as being particularly good examples of virtue," he said with an encouraging smile. "The highest sticklers are quick to censure others for their lack of propriety and not so quick to follow their own counsel. I hope you do not seek to emulate their behavior."

Alicia chuckled. "Indeed not. Mama was never so presumptuous. I recall her saying once that there was far too much fault-finding in the world and not nearly enough encouragement. She said ill-tempered folk are miserable and ought to be pitied rather than disliked."

"A wise woman," Evan commented. "Do you think perhaps she would have counseled you to forgive yourself for your error once your penance was served?"

Alicia stared at him, looking dazed. "She would have, yes." Then she took a deep breath. "But I know I would be a dreadful disappointment to her if she were here to witness it. I've been spoiled and selfish and have spoken unkindly of more than just the Duke of Wellington. And then there's my stepmother. Father asked me to make her feel at home and not only have I done the antithesis of that, but I've caused him a great deal of unpleasantness as well, since he must always mediate between the two of us."

"I can see that this pains you greatly," Evan responded, "which indicates you have the desire to alter your behavior. For your sake and that of your stepmother. For my part, I did not find much to praise about her behavior either."

"No," Alicia sighed. "We bring out the worst in each other."

"A habit," Evan counseled, "can be broken. I'm told it takes twenty-one days."

It had taken him far longer to adapt to the sedate life of a churchman after nearly two years as a wastrel, but he figured Lady Alicia had not fallen quite so far as that.

Her lips parted slightly and he was seized with a desire to touch them with his own. *What am I thinking here? I am but a clergyman to her!*

"Do you really think things could be mended between us as soon as that? But she hates me!"

Evan tilted his head to one side. "Perhaps she is only acquainted with the resentful stepdaughter. What if she were to be confronted with the real Lady Alicia, the one her mother knew she could be? Perhaps she would like *that* stepdaughter."

Alicia peered at him through narrowed eyes. "So you're saying there's a chance we might come to like each other?"

He laughed at her skeptical tone. "Perhaps. A great deal depends on her too. But as long as *you* make the effort, you will have nothing for which to castigate yourself. And chances are, your relationship with your father and your brother—when he is older—will improve as well."

She gave him an assessing look. "So you're saying that all I have to do is try to be nice to Elise for twenty-one days and then we will like each other?"

He grinned. "It's not a magic formula, my lady."

"My lady, Mr. Campbell. His Grace sent me to fetch you. Lord Stanton and Miss Campbell are ready to depart."

"Tell His Grace we are on the way," Alicia said to the maid

waiting in the doorway, who curtsied briefly and departed. "I believe we must have exceeded the quarter hour we were allotted," she told him as they made their way slowly toward the doorway. "I cannot imagine a better use of it, however. You have given me a great deal to think about, Mr. Campbell. Perhaps I shall yet be a credit to my sainted mother."

"About those sainted mothers. And fathers," he added. "They weren't that way to begin with, you know. As a matter of fact, I know quite a few who were quite devilish in their early days and then learned better."

If there's hope for one such as me, my lady, there's certainly hope for you.

As for sainthood, he himself had a l-o-n-g way to go.

Chapter Six

After seeing the guests off, Alicia's optimism began to dissipate. Without Mr. Campbell's encouragement, it was too easy to slip back into her old habit of either ignoring her stepmother or needling her into an outburst. Unfortunately, it had got to the point where she could bring out Elise's worst behavior without even trying, as today had proved. Her father had been able to maintain his composure in front of the guests, but Alicia knew from hearing raised voices emanating from her father's study that a marital squabble had resulted.

For the first time, she began to see how her own childish behavior had affected her father's marriage. At this point, she wondered whether the rift between them had become too broad to mend, even if she should be instantly removed from the household. She'd seen too many marriages in the ton where both parties despised each other and went their separate ways. In more than a few cases the father rarely saw the children and they eventually came to distrust him after hearing their mother's spiteful portrayals of his character. She did not want that for her father. Or Gervase. Or even Elise.

Marriage was for better or worse. Her own childish reaction to her stepmother could never have erased the marriage. It had only made them all miserable, especially her father. And that, she realized with growing horror, had been her primary intention all along. *He* was the one who'd pushed aside the memory of his first wife to wed someone entirely her opposite—a silly, starry-eyed debutante with an eye for a wealthy husband and a title.

Alicia realized with a start that Elise was no different from most other debutantes she knew. She'd alternately scorned and pitied them for having to wed gentlemen they disliked due to their parents' insistence on making an advantageous marriage without regard for their daughters' feelings.

Of course, Lucas Howland, the Duke of Huntingdon, was a fine figure of a man, still relatively youthful in face and figure, with a few stray silver hairs threading his dark brown locks. He lived an active lifestyle, training in boxing with Gentleman Jackson on Bond Street, and in fencing, next door, with the son of the famous Angelo. His manners were faultless, and he was known to be possessed of an amiable disposition. Who wouldn't wish to marry such an excellent gentleman?

Alicia bit her lip. Little had Elise known that along with the handsome husband, wealth and the ducal coronet came a spoiled, ungrateful stepdaughter who resented her for taking her mother's place. Not to mention servants with a tendency to look to said daughter for guidance rather than the inexperienced new mistress of the house. Perhaps she could have tried harder to make peace with her new daughter, but Alicia was by then fully grown and equally as capable of behaving in a civilized manner. Betrothed and old enough to marry, even. No doubt Elise expected the problem to disappear once the marriage was accomplished and her stepdaughter departed. No doubt she was quite overset now that said stepdaughter no longer had any marriage prospects.

Passing the nursery, she heard the laughter of a child and impulsively decided to visit her brother. Just being around him could lighten her mood. A baby's life was so much simpler, she mused. All they needed was someone to feed them, change their nappy, and show them affection, and they would respond with a joy that could lift the spirits of the most cantankerous person around.

Little Gervase, on his back being changed by his nurse, squealed with delight upon seeing her.

"Hello, little fellow," she said as she tickled his stomach. "It looks as though one person in the family is having a pleasant day."

He grabbed onto the finger she held out to him and tried to bring it to his mouth.

"Ah yes," the nurse said. "'is lordship wants everything in 'is mouth, 'e does. Once 'is teeth start comin' in, the tyke won't be so cheerful as he is today."

"Poor dear," Alicia said, lifting him up into her arms. "Such a pity you must begin the unpleasant aspects of growing up so quickly. Life is so much simpler when you are young and the adults around you manage your life for you."

"I'll take him for the nonce," she said to the nurse. "Have a cuppa if you wish. I shall call if you are needed."

The nurse bowed out and Alicia settled into the old rocker that had been soothing Howland babes for a century. "Shall we ride the horsey? Let's start with a canter, shall we?"

Supporting him under his arms, she placed him on her knee and began bobbing him up and down until he squealed with laughter. "Can you manage a gallop, I wonder?" she asked him playfully and increased the speed as she lifted him ever so slightly "out of the saddle" as her leg bounced up and down.

Finally, she lifted him up to her face, bussed him on the mouth, and cradled him tightly against her shoulder.

"You are such a sweeting," she said as she brought back down on her lap. "Just being around you would brighten anyone's day."

He beamed at her and the idea came to her. If little Gervase had such a miraculous effect on *her,* surely he would have a similar effect on his own mother!

She rose and stepped outside into the corridor.

"Do you know where I might find the duchess?" she asked a footman.

"I believe she retired to her quarters only a short time ago."

Alicia bit her lip. No doubt her stepmother was in a fine rage after her argument with her husband. Normally at such times she would do her best to avoid Elise, but that was the cowardly choice and she was determined to change her habits and attempt to mend her relationship with her stepmother.

"Don't worry, little one," she whispered to the child, "if she's not in a mood to be placated, I'll have you out of there in no time."

Elise was not in her sitting room when Alicia peered in, so she moved on and knocked hesitantly on the door of the duchess's suite.

"For goodness sake, come in and bring me my tea," said the duchess, who was lying in her large canopy bed holding a cloth to her forehead. "It's certainly taken you long enough—

"Oh, it's *you!*" she said, teeth clenched, as she perceived Alicia's presence. "What do *you* want? All of this is *your* fault, you know." Seeing Gervase, she sat up quickly.

"Is he all right? Is he feverish, do you think? Oh dear child, come to Mama and let me see you."

Alicia walked to the bed and laid him in his mother's arms. "He's fine, Elise. I didn't mean to alarm you. I just thought he might like to see his mama."

"I see," she said, continuing to stare at Alicia with suspicion in her eyes. But her expression softened when she peered into her son's eyes and he cooed with joy. "What a little darling you are!" she told him. "Yes, you are, my little marquess! A fine duke you shall be, sometime in the distant future."

"Indeed he shall be," agreed Alicia. She swallowed and added, "I know I haven't said so, Elise, but I *am* grateful to you giving my father the son he's longed for all of his life. And a brother for me, as well. I've always wanted siblings, you know. Even now that I'm quite old enough to be his mother."

Elise's eyes remained cautious. "I've—noticed that the resentment you have shown me has not been extended to my son. I-I-I feared that you might take exception to having to share your inheritance with my child."

Alicia's mouth fell open. "Heavens no!" she cried. "Never have I considered such a thing, Elise! He's my brother, the son of a duke, and is well-deserving of all that comes with it."

A sense of self-loathing came over her. "As his mother—and my father's wife—I owed you respect and consideration. Instead I greeted you with childish resentment and endeavored to make your life miserable."

She swallowed stared down at the floor.

A tap sounded and the door opened to reveal the maid with a tray. "Here you are, your grace. Cook sent up a bit of willow bark tea ease the headache— Oh, Lady Alicia! Forgive me if I've interrupted something..."

"Not at all, Brooks. Here, set the tray on this table and I'll serve Her Grace," Alicia offered.

The maid departed with a puzzled look in her eyes, and Alicia knew that the news of her presence there would be fodder for speculation below stairs.

"I owe you a thousand apologies for the way I have treated you, Elise. And my father as well. I hope to live long enough to atone for all the anguish I have caused you."

She handed a cup of tea to her stepmother, who laid the child against a pillow at her side and accepted the tea.

"I hardly know what to think," she responded after the first few sips. "Have you concluded that you've caused enough damage to my marriage and now that it's beyond repair, you can afford to show me some kindness?"

Alicia buried her face in her hands, and when she looked up again, her eyes were wet. "I deserved that," she whispered. "I have been beastly to you both. But I mean to change. For your sake and Papa's—Gervase's too. And to prove to myself that I can follow the principles with which I was raised."

Elise drained the cup and handed it back, a dazed expression on her face. "What could have brought *this* on? Was it Stanton's attachment to another woman, I wonder? I did warn you not to neglect him, you know. Even the most devoted gentleman can be lured away by a pretty face."

Alicia swallowed. She deserved that too. And much more. "You did," she agreed. "And you were right. But Milton seems quite devoted to Miss Campbell, and I think perhaps our mothers were wrong to assume that the two of us should be happy married to each other."

She handed a plate of buttered bread to her stepmother. "Would you like jam with that?"

Elise shook her head. "I really should not," she answered. "I've only just regained my shape and I have no desire to lose it again so soon."

She took a bite of the bread and regarded Alicia thoughtfully.

"Of course, you are one and twenty with no husband in sight. Could it be desperation which has prompted this change of heart? Or—" she paused to chew another bite of bread, "—could it have something to do with that handsome young vicar?"

Alicia tamped down the retort that popped into her mind.

"Oh look, Elise! Gervase has rolled himself over and is trying to crawl!"

Elise clapped her hands. "Oh he *is,* isn't he? Clever child! Although he looks much more than a snake slithering around on his stomach, doesn't he? Come here, dear boy, and give your mama a hug!"

Later that night when her head touched the pillow, Alicia recalled Elise's taunt about Mr. Campbell. Well, in a way, he *was* responsible for her change of heart. But only in a professional way, she told herself. Not in a personal way. Although he was certainly quite good-looking. And very strong, she recalled. She'd felt quite secure with his arms supporting her. And if she'd felt the tiniest bit bereft at his departure, she was certain it had more to do with the clumsiness of the aged footman who replaced him than the feeling of emptiness and loss she felt when he was gone.

The man was a vicar, for heaven's sake!

* * *

8 December 1817
En route to Huntingdon Manor

"I still say a dressmaker's shop is no place for a gentleman," Evan complained as the cart neared the drive to Huntingdon Manor. Your precious Stanton managed to worm his way out of it, after all."

Ellen jabbed him in the side with her elbow. "He had to go to Norwich on business today, and well you know it, brother dear. It's only been a few days since Lady Alicia's foot was injured; I'm sure it is only prudent to have a gentleman along to offer his assistance if required."

Evan's breath quickened as he recalled the response of his body to Lady Alicia's proximity. No doubt she thought of him as a spiritual advisor than anything else, but his strong physical response to her proved that he was still vulnerable to the temptations of the flesh.

"Besides," she added playfully, "a strong sort of gentleman shall be required to convey our boxes and packages to the carriage for us, and you are much stronger than that footman of theirs. And more attractive too. As your sister, I am not supposed to notice such things, but I'm sure Lady Alicia has."

"Don't be ridiculous," Evan scolded her, tamping down the frisson of excitement that went through him at the thought of Alicia's appreciation of his manly attributes. "The daughter of a duke can look as high as she wishes for a match. She'd never look twice at a mere nobody such as I."

Ellen gave him an assessing look. "How fascinating! I merely said she would not find it unpleasant to look upon you. I never meant to imply anything more than friendship. But now you mention it—and it's quite telling that you *did* mention it—I think the two of you might deal quite well together."

Evan rolled his eyes. "I have no such aspirations and you know it!" he said, although the sudden heat he felt from his cheeks seemed to prove otherwise. "But I'm sure it would ease your conscience considerably if a new gentleman were to step in and take the place of the fiancé you pinched from her."

She glared at him. "That's not fair and you know it, Evan Campbell!" But her wet eyes attested otherwise.

Evan felt like a boor. Lady Alicia had shown no signs of heartbreak at the loss of her betrothed, nor any resentment of his feelings for Ellen.

"Forgive me, Ellen. That was not well done of me."

He took her hand and squeezed it and she gave him a rueful smile.

"Nothing is ever simple in life," she said. "I suppose that is what makes it interesting."

By this time, they had reached the elegant portico, where the duke's crested carriage awaited them.

"I see we shall be traveling in style," Ellen commented as Evan helped her alight from the cart.

"Indeed. It is nearly as grand as Blackburn's," teased her brother. "You'd best get used to it, sister. In a matter of weeks, you shall be a viscountess."

Ellen gave him a dazed look. "Oh dear. Evan, I can't be a viscountess. I shan't know the first thing about it."

"Of course you can,"

The cheerful voice was Alicia's, and she was stunning in a magnificent hussar-style pelisse in navy velvet with diagonal stripes of gold braid pointing down to form a V in the center. A few strands of black hair escaped the confines of her matching blue coal scuttle bonnet trimmed with matching braid. She was being escorted by a footman—a younger one this time—and she walked with only a slight limp.

He bowed over her hand and she smiled at him with sparkling eyes.

"How kind of you to agree to accompany us, Mr. Campbell.

My father would rather be set upon by a band of rogues than set foot in a shop for ladies."

Then, turning to his sister. "Never fear, Miss Campbell. I shall teach you all I know about being a viscountess." She tittered. "I've never been one myself, of course, but I am acquainted with a few."

Ellen bit her lip. "You expected to become one after your marriage to Milton. I cannot feel at ease about displacing you, Lady-er-Alicia. You are much more qualified to become a viscountess than I."

Alicia snorted. "Oh, I have the viscountess part down pat, dear Ellen. Anyone can learn to look down their noses at lower beings and organize dinner parties. It's the marriage part that trips me up. I am far too spoiled and selfish to care for another person more than myself. Perhaps you can help your brother tutor me on that score."

Ellen shot him a questioning look and Evan explained that Alicia had expressed the desire to resolve her differences with her stepmother.

"I have progress to report," said Alicia with a shiver. "But my toes are freezing in these half-boots. Let us settle into the coach and Rogers can bring us some blankets and hot bricks."

The ladies were settled into the forward-facing seats with Evan across from them.

"Mrs. Russell's," Alicia called to the coachman, "on Market Street."

"As you wish, your ladyship," he replied. "I know the place well."

Alicia flushed as the coach jerked them forward. "It's not only me," she explained to the Campbells. "My stepmother patronizes Mrs. Russell as well."

"I do have a tendency to relieve my boredom with shopping," she said unapologetically. "Especially in the country. Mrs. Russell may not be the equal of Madame Soligny in London, but she's quite good. I believe she'll make you a creditable wedding dress, dear Ellen."

"I'm sure she will," Ellen agreed, "so long as you are able to advise me. I know little about fashion, and I should not care to disappoint Stanton on our wedding day."

Alicia snorted. "Milton wouldn't care if you were married in your shift. I've seen the way he looks at you. In any case, fashion has never been his forté."

Ellen blushed.

Evan took the opportunity to change the subject. "You said something about having progress to report, Miss Campbell?"

Alicia leaned forward and he noticed how her tawny eyes threw off golden sparks when she was excited.

"Indeed I do." She explained how she had apologized to her stepmother.

"Of course, she thought it a very bad joke at first, and she's still suspicious. I can't say I blame her. I'm afraid I've been a thorn in her side for a long time."

"It's a start," Evan said with an encouraging smile. "In time, you should see results. I'm sure Her Grace will see the advantages of being on good terms with her stepdaughter."

Alicia looked skeptical. "I do hope so, since I am unlikely to be off her hands any time soon." Then she shrugged and changed the subject.

"It occurred to me that this is my brother's first Christmas. While it is true that he is too small to care one way or the other, it occurred to me that a traditional Christmas is just what our family needs."

Her eyes grew animated. "Mama used to make Christmas such a memorable time by following all the old traditions. She always said it was important to keep our forebears in mind at least once a year by keeping to their ways of celebrating the Yule.

"It is already Advent, of course, so the Christmas pudding should have been started a fortnight ago, but I persuaded Cook to help me mix up a batch yesterday after church. And I got everyone in the household to stir it—for good luck, you know—including Gervase, although Elise had to help him. So, we are expecting 1818 to be a very good year indeed!"

She beamed at Evan and then her eyes widened. "Oh! That is just superstition, of course. I hope that does not offend you, Mr. Campbell."

"Not at all, my lady. The Yuletide traditions tend to be more pagan than Christian, but I find them quite harmless and even helpful in bringing families together to celebrate the birth of Our Lord."

"Our family always anticipated the Christmas holidays," added Ellen. "Evan and I stirred our Christmas pudding a fortnight ago. And the Blackburn household as well," she said, blushing. "I thought it would cheer up the earl to see the old traditions return. Nobody bothered, you see, after Lady Blackburn died."

"Indeed, I'm sure it must be a great comfort for him to see the Court restored to life with the prospect of a new bride," Alicia conjectured. "You must get Mrs. Berry to make up a pot of the late Lady Blackburn's wassail. Mama was the only one with whom she shared the recipe, and we always had it warming on the hearth at the Manor for any visitors who happened to call."

* * *

Alicia thoroughly enjoyed the company of the Campbells on the short journey to the modiste. Ellen's eyes sparkled with happiness as she spoke of the wedding and her fiancé, and it was clear that it was he she loved and not his title or wealth. Milton was a lucky man to have found a woman who adored him. Ellen's charm went beyond her dark good looks. She was truly a sweet-tempered young woman well-grounded in her faith, but in an upbeat way as opposed to the dourness of the pious women Alicia had met. She would be a perfect wife for Milton and viscountess—eventually countess.

Alicia felt like a silly child in comparison.

"Are you all right, Lady Alicia?"

Mr. Campbell must have noticed her sudden frown.

She cleared her throat. "I was just thinking that your sister will make a much better countess than I would have done. Milton is a fortunate man indeed to have found her."

The two of them stared at her.

Ellen was the first to find her voice. "What a ridiculous thing to say, Lady Alicia! Why, you know more in your little finger about being a viscountess than I shall ever know!"

Alicia waved a hand across her chest. "Anyone can learn to make calls and pour tea. It's far more difficult to be a generous and truly unselfish person such as you are, Miss Campbell. As my mother was," she added softly.

The conversation was fortunately interrupted when the carriage stopped in front of Mrs. Russell's shop. Alicia avoided Mr. Campbell's gaze as he helped her alight from the carriage. She knew they both wanted to continue the conversation but hoped that the excitement of handling fabrics and furbelows would erase the subject from their minds. She didn't wish to be pitied, after all.

"Campbell! Evan Campbell! Is that you, man? I vow it's been years since I've seen you last! Where was it? Ma Creighton's establishment on Wimpole Street, I believe! You were with the buxom redhead—Nell."

The speaker wobbled toward them, a shabbily dressed, not-so-young-looking gentleman who was obviously the worse for drink.

Mr. Campbell's face tightened. "Be gone, Simpson! There are ladies here!"

The drunkard's eyes widened. "Ladies? And very lovely ladies they are, too! Won't you share one with an old friend? I'll gladly take the taller one off yer hands!"

Mr. Campbell turned a grim face to the ladies.

"My apologies, ladies. I'll deal with him as soon as you are both safely inside the shop."

Alicia turned a questioning face at Ellen as they were ushered unceremoniously into the shop.

Ellen shook her head. "My brother wasn't *always* a man of God," she said as they both watched from the window as Evan planted the interloper a whopper of a facer. "Occasionally his past comes back to haunt him."

Mr. Campbell returned and set up guard in the reception area as the ladies turned their attention to fabrics and lace.

But Alicia yearned to know more about the fascinating Mr. Campbell. A vicar with a past! What had brought him back into the fold?

Chapter Seven

10 December 1817
Huntingdon Manor

"That makes two dozen jars of currant jelly, and thirty of apple for today," Alicia said, running a hand over her perspiring forehead. "With the strawberry jam Cook put up in August and the raspberry from Blackburn Court, we should have more than enough for both our tenants and Blackburn's, as well as for the poor of the Castle Acre and East Winch parishes."

"We'll have hams from Blackburn Court, but Mrs. Berry and the kitchen staff will be too busy with the preparations for the wedding breakfast to do much else."

Ellen bit her lip. "Perhaps a Christmas wedding was not the best of ideas. I wonder if we shouldn't postpone it after all."

Alicia took her hand and squeezed it. "Nonsense. The wedding must go forward. It's for Blackburn's sake, remember? How is the earl doing, by the way? I hope the excitement is not proving too much for him."

Ellen fingered the cross on the chain around her neck. "He tries to put on a good face, but the doctor says his time is running out. Milton wanted to get a special license just in case, but the earl insists on it being a Christmas wedding."

Her shoulders quaked. "It's so very draining, you know. Planning a wedding... and a funeral... all at the same time. I don't know what I should do without you, Alicia. I'm sure I couldn't have dealt with the Christmas obligations on top of everything."

Alicia pulled out a chair and motioned for her to sit down. "Some tea and crumpets, Cook, if you please. And some clotted cream if you have any."

"Right away, my lady. Byers, take these jars into the pantry for now. Gates, set up tea for the ladies."

"Right here in the kitchen, ma'am?"

"That's wot I said, Gates." The heavyset, friendly-faced cook crossed her arms. "Yer new, or ye'd know that Lady Alicia has always had the run 'o the kitchen. Taught 'r to make those raspberry tarts 'er ma was so fond of."

The young maid nodded and set about preparing tea for the ladies.

Ellen tilted her head to the side.

"You intrigue me, Alicia. Before we met, Milton told me you were not the toplofty sort, but I would never have expected you to feel at home in a kitchen. Much less learn to bake and make preserves in one!"

Alicia snorted. "Do not be deceived. The household would starve if it depended on my cooking. But Mama thought a young lady should be conversant with the way a household is run, and that includes the kitchen.

"Thank you, Gates." She picked up the teapot and poured tea into two cups. "Sugar? Milk?"

"Both, please."

Ellen took a sip of tea and set her cup down. "You don't give yourself enough credit, you know. You didn't have to befriend me, you know. Under the circumstances, it would not have been thought exceptional for you to avoid me."

Alicia gave a self-deprecating laugh. "Oh, I couldn't do that."

"Why not? Some would say I robbed you of your fiancé."

Alicia took a bite of the scone Gates had set down before her.

"Milton and I go back a long way. He loves you in a way we never loved each other. I'm sure that has something to do with the reason we kept postponing our wedding."

"But you never met another gentleman you liked better?"

Alicia shrugged. "I never really thought about it," she lied. She'd been thinking a great deal about a certain handsome vicar of her acquaintance. But that was just curiosity about his past. Wasn't it?

"Because you were betrothed," Ellen persisted. "Now you must begin again. Unless you wish to remain with your father and stepmother forever."

Alicia took another sip of tea. "Not that!" she said dramatically. "A fate worse than death! Although," she continued after swallowing another bite of scone, "Elise and I have come to a truce. She's been under the weather and I offered to take over the preparations for Christmas this year. That's how I got the idea to enlist your help."

"*My* help?" Ellen rolled her eyes. "It's quite the other way round, my dear. My head is spinning with all that is happening at Blackburn Court and I should never have managed the Boxing Day gifts for the tenants without you to advise me. In fact," she said, staring at her empty palms, "I could not have helped my brother with the visits to the poor without your help either. There are times when," she said in a quaking voice, "I feel certain I shall turn out a simply dreadful viscountess!"

"Wedding jitters. You'll get over them. If you want to become Milton's wife, you will, that is. Do you?"

"Of course!" Ellen's eyes shone. "That is all that is important, is it not?"

She eyed Alicia with a pensive expression on her face. "You know, Alicia, you really are quite a remarkable person. No, don't protest. You've made some mistakes in the past, as we all have, but you have owned up to them and set about making amends with a vengeance.

"You remind me a great deal of Evan. Both of you haunted by the mistakes of the past. It's over! Time to move on with the rest of your life."

She reached across the table to take both of Alicia's hands. "Though your sins be as scarlet, they shall be as white as snow.

"God has forgiven you, Alicia. Now you must forgive yourself."

* * *

16 December 1817
Huntingdon Manor

"Alicia dear, could you come in for a moment, please?"

Her father stood in the doorway of his study. In shirt sleeves, so he must have been working.

"Of course, Papa."

She had just returned from a trip to the modiste's, where both she and Ellen were fitted for their wedding clothes. Ellen's gown would be ivory satin with white lace and gold trim. Alicia could have worn any of the dozens of gowns in her wardrobe, but rationalized that her best friend's wedding deserved something new, and so had ordered an olive green silk gown with matching netting, with gold ribbon under her bosom.

Handing her cloak and muff to the butler and her bonnet to the footman, she smiled as she strolled over to her father and stepped up to kiss him on the cheek.

"What is it, Papa? Is it Elise?"

Her father ushered her into the room and closed the door.

"She's breeding again. I'm sure you've guessed by now. We wanted to tell you together, but between one thing and another—her being so ill most of the time—we just never managed it."

Alicia ran and embraced him, her eyes sparkling. "Congratulations, Papa! I'm so happy for you!" She grinned. "And for me. To have another little brother or sister as darling as dear Gervase!"

She took his arm and led him to a brown leather chair, then seated herself nearby. "I did suspect, of course. She was so miserably ill in those first months when she was expecting Gervase." She swallowed. "I recall behaving quite churlishly at the time, which made it all the worse for her. That was not well done of me, I know, Papa."

The duke shook his head. "No, no. What's past is past, my dear. That's not why I called you in here. Although I did want to commend you on your efforts in making overtures to my wife of late. Particularly with your offer to manage the Christmas preparations. She is very appreciative, my dear. We both are."

Alicia fidgeted. "It's really nothing, Papa. After all, what else have I to do? Everyone around me is inundated with tasks related to Christmas, weddings, estates, tenants." She stared down at her hands. "All while the earl's life hangs on by a thread. I couldn't very well spend my time embroidering cushions, could I?"

Her father swallowed. "Indeed not. The earl has been a good friend to me... to us all. It is difficult to imagine a world without him in it." He turned warm eyes to her. "I'm quite proud of you, my dear, for getting over your disappointment over the betrothal and showing your support so openly for the couple. That will surely squelch any hint of scandal."

"Oh, I didn't do it for that, Papa. Ellen is a sweet girl and Milton deserves her. I hope we shall all be lifelong friends." She grinned. "And it's fun planning a wedding. I'm having a new gown made for the occasion, after all."

Her father leaned back and sighed deeply. "You remind me so much of your mother, you know. She would be so proud of what you have become, my dear." Then he straightened up. "But that's not what I wanted to speak to you about either."

He reached into his pocket and pulled out a letter. "This is from your Aunt Beatrice. She is traveling to Paris next month and has invited you to join her." He shook his head. "Apparently the news of your broken betrothal has already hit the London circuit and she believes you might find an eligible *partie* there since you haven't thus far in London circles."

Alicia felt disoriented. "Paris?"

She'd always yearned to go to Paris. The wide boulevards. The châteaux. Art. Fashions. Elaborate drawing rooms. Salon hostesses. The whole experience. Now that the war was well over, Paris was *the* place to be. And now her aunt was giving her the opportunity to do it all.

Perhaps to find an elegant *comte* or *marquis* who would marry her and take her away to a magnificent château in the country to host lavish balls and raise little *comtes* and *comtesses* and have the world at her beck and call.

Why didn't that sound so appealing to her?

"Of course, you'll have to have a whole new wardrobe done while you're there," her father said with a twinkle. "Your aunt has warned me that the price will be steep."

Alicia managed a feeble smile. "How... generous of you, Papa!"

"She plans to leave a week or so after Twelfth Night," her father continued. "As long as the weather cooperates, that is. Shall I write to her to accept, or would you prefer to do so yourself?"

Alicia took the letter from his hands. "I'll do it, Papa. As soon as I can arrange it."

But her heart was heavy as she headed upstairs to her bedchamber. Paris, with all its wealth and glamor and scintillating personalities, could not hold a candle to the real life she was living in her own home. It was a fairy tale, like her life in London had been. And she was done with fairy tales. She wanted her life to mean something. Settle down and raise a family and teach her children to be thoughtful and responsible and helpful to others. Be a helpmate and partner to her husband, as Ellen would be.

But Ellen had a husband. She did not. And where would she find a suitable match in this neck of the woods?

The darkly handsome face of the vicar appeared in her head,

but she shook it away. She could never be a vicar's wife. Evan Campbell would look for someone who could manage a home with only one servant at most. And she was hardly the type to lead sewing circles and prayer groups.

No, perhaps she would have to go to Paris after all. Pity she couldn't work up any enthusiasm for it.

* * *

Thursday, December 18, 1817
Castle Acre Parish

"Perhaps you should allow me to do this one, Lady Alicia. The Harrises' cottage is little more than a hovel, and I'm afraid it might shock your ladylike sensibilities," suggested Evan with a teasing smile.

"Fiddlesticks! I've no more ladylike sensibilities than you, Mr. Campbell. And it's Alicia, remember? Milton is my brother in spirit and your sister is to become his wife. We're family now. No more of this lady nonsense."

She was substituting for Ellen, who was busy wedding planning at Blackburn Court, in the delivery of baskets for the parish poor.

She turned to face him, her expression serious. "What is their situation? Is Mr. Harris a drunkard like Ned Bates?"

Evan grimaced. Ned Bates's family existed on the edge of poverty due to his inability to remain employed. His gardening skills should have assured him a decent position; however, he was belligerent and unreliable when drunk, which was most of the time. Alicia had spoken at length with Mrs. Bates and the fourteen-year-old daughter and offered to find the girl a place on the staff in a good home.

The Bates children were reasonably clean and showed no sign of abuse, although they were on the thin side. Mrs. Bates had accepted the box of food with gratitude, and when Alicia afterward asked what else was being done to help the family, Evan had explained that he gave the children food in exchange for caring for the church grounds and cemetery, but that any money they received was always confiscated by Ned and used to feed his addiction to gin or rum or whatever was around at the time.

The Bateses were actually the poorest family in the parish. Evan saw the concern in Alicia's eyes and felt instantly sorry for teasing her.

"Forgive me, your ladyship—er—Alicia. I am a cad for baiting you. The Harrises are two middle-aged spinsters whose father is a butler who was recently pensioned off by his employer. The ladies supplement their income by taking in sewing, but that won't be much to live on once the father passes on and they are evicted from the cottage."

Alicia's eyes, which had narrowed at his admission of guilt, quickly changed to concern at hearing the sisters' plight.

"Is that likely to happen soon? Where would they go?"

Evan shook his head. "They may have distant relatives somewhere who will take them in as dependents, but it's unlikely they would be suitable servants."

"Why not?"

Evan tilted his head and shrugged as he led her up to the cottage, which was in decent shape, albeit in need of a coat of paint.

"Papa, Mae, it's the vicar come ta visit! An' a beauteeful lady. Welcome, yer majesty. Do ye be a duchess?"

Alicia shot him a piqued look as they were ushered into the cottage, which was clean, but small and crude, consisting of one room with a curtained off area where a sturdy pale woman in gray —an exact copy of the odd-faced woman who had answered the door—appeared to be tending to someone in a bed.

"Good morning, Miss Fae and Miss Mae. And Mr. Dawson, how are you doing today? This is Lady Alicia Howland, daughter of the Duke of Huntingdon over in East Winch. She has graciously agreed to assist me in distributing the Parish Christmas boxes this year."

"Papa's middlin' this day," Mae said as she pulled the curtain open to reveal the wizened old man in the bed, who appeared to be trying to sit up.

"Beg your pardon, my lady," said Mr. Dawson in a weak voice. "Should show... obeisance..."

Alicia's eyes widened in horror. "Oh no, please do not get up, Mr. Dawson. You must not risk your health."

The first twin—for that is obviously what they were—had opened the box and exclaimed excitedly over its contents.

"Biscuits! Lots of 'em, Mae! A nice ham, too. And jam." She squealed. "Ham and jam! Ham and jam! And bread. Two whole loaves!"

Mae's eyes lit up and she joined her sister in rummaging through the box.

"Mind your manners, Daughters," their father said as authoritatively as he could in his weakened condition. "Put the box down and thank her ladyship and the vicar for their kindness."

Chastened, the twins did as they were told, curtsying awkwardly to their guests.

"Please... stay for tea," the old man coughed out.

While his daughters prepared the tea, Mr. Dawson confided his worries for his offspring after his death.

"They can take care of themselves, do mending, that sort of thing. But without a home, they'll surely go to the workhouse. Wouldn't last long there." He closed his eyes briefly as a another coughing fit attacked him.

"Nice, obedient girls," he managed to get out. "Deserve better."

Evan assured him that he and the Parish Committee would try to find a way to keep his daughters from the workhouse, and later, as they returned to the coach, Alicia turned worried eyes toward him.

"What can be done for them? Who would have the heart to evict them? It's only a simple cottage, after all."

Evan explained that the cottage was owned by Owen Rutledge, a wealthy landowner.

"Dawson has worked for the family over sixty years and has earned his pension, but the Rutledges aren't known for their generosity. His attention seems to be elsewhere whenever the necessity for a new roof on the church is mentioned."

Alicia's hands clenched. "But... these are *people!* And it's so little, really. How could anyone be so hard-hearted?"

"No doubt it seems so to us. But there are many in this world who do not believe the poor deserve to be helped. 'He helps them who help themselves' and all that."

Alicia glared at him. "But-But that's outrageous! What if they *can't* help themselves?"

She was flushed with anger, and Evan was taken aback at the vehemence of her response. This was no society lightweight with no thought in her head other than what dress to wear and what gentleman to flirt with. Was this Alicia the real one or was this simply a passing fancy to her?

"There are some who believe it is enough to teach them to recite Bible verses in the hope that they will draw on their faith to get them through their tribulations," he told her as he assisted her into the coach. "And others who are of the opinion that the poor are being punished for either their own acts or those of their forebears."

"That's the last." He called to the coachman. "Return me to the vicarage and with luck you'll get back to Huntingdon before the storm."

"Aye, sir," responded the coachman doubtfully as he eyed the dark clouds overhead.

Alicia's hand flew to her chest as she peered out the window. "A storm?"

"Looks like it," Evan said grimly. "And given the chill in the air, there will likely be snow and ice."

The road was already icy by the time they pulled up in front of the Castle Acre vicarage. The horses's manes were covered with snow and the coachman hopped down from his perch to check their condition and toss a worried look at the nearly invisible road along with Evan, who had likewise descended, and Alicia, who leaned her head out of the doorway.

"Best not to tax the horses in this weather," Evan advised. "Not after the effort they've put in today. Take them to the inn stables for a rubdown and some oats, and then join Lady Alicia and me for a meal. I'd invite you to the vicarage," he said with a smile at Alicia, "but my sister is away for the day and it wouldn't do to set the village tabbies' mouths afire. Besides, I'm an appalling cook and Mrs. Ferguson sets a fine table. If you like good English cooking."

"Aye, she does," agreed the coachman. "Scots fare too. Her neeps 'n tatties are the best to be found outside of bonnie Scotland herself."

"Ah, neeps 'n tatties," said Evan. "Are you fond of Scots fare, Lady Alicia?"

"I've never been," Alicia said with a curious look at Evan. "Are you, Mr. Campbell? Scottish, I mean."

Evan grinned. "My father grew up in Inverness. Moved to Norwich to live with English relatives when his parents died. Complained about English food so much my mother learned to cook Scots food for special occasions. I've never had better haggis from anyone, although Mrs. Ferguson's is quite tasty."

* * *

Haggis, as Alicia was to discover, was a type of savory pudding containing the entrails of sheep minced with onion, oatmeal, and suet, among other things, and cooked for hours while encased in a sheep's stomach.

"A sheep's stomach?" she echoed doubtfully. "I suppose it could be no worse than mince pie or blood pudding."

"Believe me, Lady Alicia," he said as they were giving the order to the innkeeper's wife, "it is really quite delicious, particularly Mrs. Ferguson's version."

Mrs. Ferguson beamed and Alicia forced a smile. "I should love to try it," she said. "And some of the other—what was it, Mr. Campbell? Neeps and something?"

Neeps turned out to be turnips and tatties were cooked potatoes smashed up and stirred with butter and salt. After a tentative bite of the haggis, she gave a squeal of surprise and turned to Evan with wide eyes.

"It doesn't taste at all like sheep's stomach," she said. "But I can't think of anything else that it resembles either. It's delicious!"

Evan burst out laughing. "Haggis is a culinary specialty of its own," he said proudly. "Perhaps if we English were to eat it we'd be much less stiff-rumped and more spontaneous and hot-blooded, like the Highlanders."

Alicia noticed how his dark eyes sparkled with warmth and congeniality while he spoke of his father's heritage.

"Does that mean you consider yourself more Scots than English? Do you really believe *we* are rather staid in comparison?" she asked as she reached for the glass of ale in front of her.

He stared at her speculatively. "Perhaps. Although the Scots can be quite staid—or stiff-rumped—themselves on occasion."

"But there's a certain fiery passion associated with the Scots, isn't there? With the Highlanders at least. When you picture them rushing downhill to attack Cumberland's forces at Culloden, all red beards and tartans bearing claymores and making a dreadful clamor to frighten the enemy out of their wits."

"Passion. Aye, they had that," said Mrs. Ferguson grimly as she advanced to refill their tankards. "But not much luck. Not that day or since."

"Oh dear, forgive me. I wasn't thinking..." Alicia mentally berated herself for her thoughtlessness.

Mrs. Ferguson shrugged. "It's been a long time, my lady. Things is wot they is. No use mournin' the past."

She bustled back into the kitchen.

Alicia set her tankard down and smiled. "Mama used to say that. Or something like. 'It is what it is.' She told me it makes no sense to hold grudges or mourn forever for the past. She said it was the extreme act of selfishness to allow the past to hold sway over the rest of your life."

Evan tilted his head and gave her a questioning look.

"I must confess I hadn't thought of it in quite that way."

Alicia leaned forward. "She gave the example of her grandmother, who was abandoned by her husband and lived the rest of her life shut up in the country with only servants for company. The few times Mama saw her, she was dressed in mourning and did nothing but bemoan the past and criticize everyone for ignoring her. But who wants to be around someone like that? Her self-centered behavior deprived her children of a mother and her grandchildren of a grandmother."

Alicia rolled her eyes. "After a while, nobody could blame her husband for abandoning her, no matter that he was a bounder. In the end, she wasted her entire life for nothing."

"Indeed," Evan responded as he studied Alicia's eyes. "The mistakes of the past cannot be changed, but that doesn't mean the future must be colored by them. That was the original purpose of the confessional—to encourage people to admit their sins, be reassured that they are forgiven, and continue on with their lives."

"Perhaps the confessional should be brought back," Alicia suggested. "I know that I feel a great deal better since confessing my own sins and resolving to do better in future."

"Perhaps," he said with a strange look in his eye. "But it isn't really necessary to tell another person, is it? And imagine the priest having to hear everyone's sins and have them roaming around in his head at every moment of the day. As a man of the cloth," he added as he attacked the last of his haggis, "I am exceedingly grateful that the confessional was abolished all those years ago."

He had secrets. Ellen had hinted the same, and Alicia could

see it in his eyes. But it was also clear that he wasn't ready to speak about them, and there seemed no point in pressing him.

"Perhaps a change of subject is in order," she said with a cheery smile. "Regarding the wedding clothing—you *will* have a white waistcoat for the wedding breakfast, will you not? I understand that as the officiating minister your dress is prescribed, but as the brother of the bride, your apparel should resemble that of the other gentlemen."

They argued companionably until the meal was over and then settled down before the fire until at last the coachman informed them that the snow had finally ceased.

"Are you certain the roads are passable? I shouldn't like to send her ladyship into danger," Evan said, wrinkling his brow.

"I just came from Swaffham and the road is decent if ye take it slow," volunteered a bearded man who had entered along with the coachman. "Lynn Road's clear. Didn't snow much a'tall in Narborough or East Winch."

"There's still enough daylight ta make it if we leave now, my lady," said the coachman. "Wouldn't want His Grace to fret any if ye don't return this eve."

"Thank you, Forbes. I shall be along directly."

Although to be honest, Alicia was reluctant to leave. The inn was warm and comfortable, the food decent, and the company—well, she adored being in Evan's company. He was as charming and amusing as any gentleman she'd met, and not at all stodgy and boring as she'd come to expect men of God to be. He liked helping people—and she did as well—and she could see him as an excellent husband and father one day. Just the sort of man she'd like to marry herself.

One day.

"Don't forget—we're expecting you at the Manor on Christmas Eve along with the bridal couple. It's my first dinner party, but I promise not to poison you," she said as she accepted his assistance in entering the coach.

"We shall not disappoint you," he promised.

Mistletoe, she said to herself as they drove away. There shall definitely be a few appropriately-placed sprigs of mistletoe for the occasion.

Chapter Eight

December 24, 1817
Huntingdon Manor

"You are certain the table is set properly, Mrs. Cross? Is the centerpiece too tall, do you think? Oh, I do wish I had paid more attention to the details at all the dinners I've attended! I never realized there was so much involved when it was all done by another."

The housekeeper smiled and patted her on the shoulder. "No need to worry, my lady. It's not *my* first dinner. Nor even the new footman's, since he came to us from the Binghams in King's Lynn. We have a first-class staff here at the Manor. And ye've done a wonderful job with the menu and the decorations." She wiped her eyes with the corner of her apron. "I haven't seen the Manor so festive since—since—"

"Since Mama died." Alicia blinked at the tears in her own eyes. "I own that thought has occurred to me as well, Mrs. Cross. Although I'm sure the new duchess would have done as well had she been in health the past two Christmases."

"Alicia, my dear, your father is ready to toast the happy couple," came the voice of her stepmother. "Do come and welcome them as tonight's hostess."

Elise looked lovely in her red velvet holiday gown with a matching bow embellishing her pale blonde hair.

"Isn't that the gown you intend to wear for the wedding? I'm quite sure it is bad luck to wear it a day ahead of time—" She bit her lip, "but that is only superstition, of course. You do look well in it, of course. And the green is so Christmassy too. Especially with my red. Come along, Daughter, and let us welcome our special guests."

Alicia wanted to chuckle at Elise's use of "daughter" in conjunction with herself. She couldn't remember that ever happening before. While she doubted she could ever think of Elise in any maternal way, she was gratified that they had reached a truce—no, more of an accord—and that the improved ambience had affected all of the Howlands in a positive way. Her father seemed happier and more relaxed than she had ever seen him, and she and Elise no longer squabbled over Gervase, who was always delighted to see both of them.

She joined the party in the drawing room just in time to see Milton take his bride in his arms and give her a big, smacking kiss under the mistletoe that hung in front of the fireplace.

"Hear hear!" applauded her father as the couple pulled apart and Milton proudly displayed his blushing bride, who was wearing a gold silk gown that was *not* her wedding gown. "Time for the toast!"

"Wait!" Elise said as she hurried to the door to greet a gaily dressed Gervase, being carried by his nurse. "Gervase is here to wish the happy couple well. Come, my darling."

She picked him up in her arms and took him to his father, who slung him up to his left shoulder and motioned for Alicia to join them.

"It is written, when their children find true love, their parents find true joy," he said as he waved an arm in the direction of the happy couple. "Stanton here has always been a son to me, long before I ever had one of my own—" He grinned at Gervase, who seemed to be fascinated by the diamond pin on his lapel. "Blackburn could not be with us this evening, and in his absence, I am delighted to claim him and his lovely bride as honorary Howlands from this day forward."

Alicia and Evan reached at the same time for a flute of champagne from the tray offered by the new footman and they both smiled. Evan was looking handsome in a black frock coat with a white waistcoat and a cravat tied in the waterfall style. He looked as fine as any gentleman of the ton, she thought, and gave him further credit for having no valet to assist.

"Here's to the health and happiness of the happy couple," said her father, and they moved forward to clink their glasses and drink their champagne.

The guests of honor led the procession into the dining room, followed by the Huntingdons, who handed Gervase back to his nurse, with Alicia and Evan bringing up the rear.

Alicia was buzzing with excitement for the evening. There was a sense of accomplishment for her efforts in planning the event—along with a certain amount of anxiety that some disaster might occur. But she forgot all of it when she looked into her escort's eyes and saw a light in them that made her catch her breath.

"You look lovely this evening, Lady Alicia. The green brings out the gold lights in your eyes."

Alicia's heart hammered in her chest. Goodness! She'd been flattered with much more poetic compliments and never experienced such agitation. But then... she'd never cared so much about the gentlemen who uttered them as she did about this one.

"I see you *do* have a white waistcoat," she whispered back.

"My only sister is marrying an earl's heir tomorrow, and I wouldn't wish to disgrace her."

Alicia pointed her head toward the table, where Milton was carefully seating his bride at the place of honor at the duke's right hand. "I don't believe *she* cares particularly *what* you wear. Nor Milton either. Do you see the way they are looking at each other? I'm sure they are wishing the rest of us far away."

He gave her a meaningful look before they reached the table

and he pulled out her chair for her before being seated in his own by the new footman, who, Alicia was glad to see, did seem to have a good grasp of his duties.

As a matter of fact, *all* of the Huntingdon servants performed admirably. The dinner table, painstakingly set with the best china, crystal and silver, and strewn with lengths of holly and ivy, was lit by a dozen wax candles set in candelabras that had been gifts from the King for her parents' wedding more than two decades earlier.

From the turtle soup to the roast goose, the food was excellent and well-received, and finally, Alicia was able to relax and concentrate on her guests. After the dainty strawberry tarts were served with candied cherries and clotted cream, the duke rose and announced that the gentlemen would forego their port to adjourn to the drawing room with the ladies. As they all rose from their chairs, he added.

"The duchess has informed me that the credit for tonight's dinner goes to my daughter, who insisted on making all of the arrangements in honor of the bond between our two families for several generations."

Alicia blushed at the acclamation. "It makes me very happy to honor my best friend upon his marriage and welcome his bride and her brother into the family."

Turning to Ellen and Milton: "I hope we shall remain friends and thus will our mothers' fond wishes be realized."

She turned her gaze on Evan, and realized she didn't want to be his friend. Nor was she still thinking he would make some lucky woman a fine husband.

She wanted to *be* that lucky woman.

* * *

Friends? She wanted to be his friend?

But she reddened when she looked at him and quickly looked away, and Evan had a sudden notion that it wasn't friendship she had in mind and a flutter of hope galvanized to action in his belly.

She smiled and took his arm when he offered it, and they all retired to the drawing room, where they settled down next to each other on a settee near the back of the room.

His sister and Lady Huntingdon chatted about wedding minutiae while the duke and Stanton discussed the harvest and other estate matters.

"Are you responsible for the festive decor, Lady Alicia?"

She fidgeted. "I merely directed the servants. My stepmother hasn't been feeling well—she's expecting a child in the summer, you know. It was my duty to help." She looked up and feigned a frown. "And it's Alicia. I thought we had moved beyond the formalities."

Evan temporarily forgot to breathe. She was so lovely and so close he could see her chest rise and fall with each breath. Her eyes were flashing gold sparks at him, and her lips appeared so full and soft he was sorely tempted to kiss them, damn propriety to hell!

He smiled. "True, but with your father here and in such elegant surroundings... I thought it best to play it safe."

She raised her eyebrows. "Indeed, Papa can be quite formidable in his ducal guise, but it is not his normal mien. In other words," she leaned toward him and whispered, "he doesn't bite. Not usually, anyway."

"—My wife is fatigued and I am certain you young people are not ready to call it an evening. You will take over as host, will you not, Alicia, my dear?"

They both started at the duke's words.

"Of course, Papa. Good night. Sleep well."

She turned to the bridal couple. "Can I get you anything? Tea? Champagne? More tarts?"

Milton and Ellen exchanged glances, and Milton cleared his throat.

"It is kind of you to offer, Alicia, but if you don't mind, I should like to show my bride the gallery before we part for the evening."

The gallery? So late at night? Not to look at old portraits, that's for sure.

Alicia bit her lip and rose to ring for a servant.

"I'll get a lamp and accompany you," she said, her eyes twinkling at Evan.

Milton seized a candelabra from the mantel. "Oh—that won't be necessary, Alicia dear."

Ellen nudged him in the side. "Er—we shan't be gone long," she said apologetically. "Although..." she added with an uneasy look, "perhaps these two should not be left alone, my dear."

Milton winked at them. "They'll be fine. Your brother is a man of God, after all. And, as you say, we shan't be gone long enough for anything improper to occur."

"If you say so, my love," Ellen said, looking up at him with her heart in her eyes.

"We'll leave the door ajar." And with that, they fled the room and muffled giggles could be heard as they darted up the stairs.

Evan and Alicia looked at each other.

"I wonder what they think we shall do," Alicia said, clasping her hands together.

"Do you really?" Evan teased. Her face was slightly flushed, but she raised her eyes to his as though looking for him to take the next step.

"I think they are expecting us to do... this," he said as his fingers gently bent her head toward his and kissed her.

After a brief start of surprise, she kissed him with an intensity that surprised him. She leaned forward and gripped his shoulders to draw them closer together. Evan's heart hammered in his chest and all he was aware of was the euphoria of having the woman he loved in his arms, responding to his kiss. He wanted desperately to deepen the kiss, to run his fingers through her hair, revel in the softness of her skin, and make her his. But he could not. Not now. For so many reasons.

But maybe... someday soon. The softness in her eyes and the

way she melted in his arms gave him hope that she returned his feelings.

The kiss ended and he removed her hands from his shoulders and clasped them in his own hands.

"I'm glad," she said, with a tremulous smile.

"That we kissed?"

"That, yes, and that they gave us a moment of privacy."

She moistened her lips and a sudden jolt of desire reverberated through his body.

"Was there something in particular you wished to say to me?"

She gave him a look of mock exasperation and jabbed him in the side with her elbow.

"No... yes. I thought perhaps we might have something to say *to each other.*"

Ah, he thought. The lady cannot speak first. It was up to him. And yet... she was a duke's daughter. He resolutely pushed that thought aside. She was Alicia. The woman he loved. If she returned his feelings, the rest didn't matter. Did it?

He took her hands back in his and squeezed them gently as he looked into her eyes. "My dear Alicia, it seems my feelings of admiration for you have deepened into something considerably more serious. If... you feel you may someday reciprocate, I would like to ask permission to court you." He took a deep breath. "If my request is displeasing to you, please do say so now and I promise we will remain friends as before."

"You want to court me? Oh, Evan!"

She threw her arms around his neck. "Yes! Yes! I do love you, Evan!"

Any remnant of doubt flew out of Evan's mind. This time he deepened the kiss and moved his hands to her back to draw her closer. She responded eagerly, her pulse racing along with his. A hand crept to the side of her breast, and a slight hesitation from her brought him back to reality.

She was innocent. Her responses were passionate, yet untutored, and he perceived that she had not gone so far with any other gentleman. A fact which pleased him greatly. But *they* were not being married tomorrow. The affection between them had happened so quickly... too quickly. She deserved a proper courtship, if only to allow her—both of them—time to validate their feelings for each other.

He ended the kiss and set her aside gently. She blinked.

"Oh my!"

Her face was flushed and she promptly set about straightening her clothing, avoiding his eyes.

He touched her cheek and drew her head back to face him.

"I love kissing you, and I hope to spend the rest of my life showing you how much, but until I speak to your father, it wouldn't be proper to take further advantage of you."

She smiled and licked her lips, and he felt a jolt that went straight to his groin.

"Perhaps tomorrow—" and then she caught her breath. "The wedding. And Christmas. I almost forgot!" Her eyes widened and she giggled. "How quickly such unimportant things fly out of my mind when you are close to me!"

Evan pressed his lips together. "I should not wish your father to perceive that our feelings are merely a result of wedding fervor. Perhaps the following day..."

"Boxing Day. You and I are slated to disburse the boxes to the tenants of both estates that day, remember? Perhaps you could come to dinner after and we could speak to Papa."

"An excellent plan." But the thought of what he would say to the duke put his head temporarily in a spin. What did one say at such a time to allay the duke's fears that he was an upstart and fortune hunter? If their places were switched and a penniless vicar with a murky pass were to dare ask for the hand of *his* daughter, he'd send him on his way directly.

Which reminded him that Alicia didn't know of his past. He owed that to her. She might be willing to make a mésalliance for love, but she should do so with full knowledge of his disreputable history.

But when? Not tonight. He didn't wish to spoil the moment. Not tomorrow either. Perhaps on Boxing Day, after they had finished their rounds and were enjoying wassail in front of the fire.

The clock struck midnight and they turned to each other and said, "Happy Christmas!"

And then it occurred that they hadn't made use of the kissing bough yet, so he stood and pulled her toward the fireplace, where he pointed over their heads and their lips met.

"Ah hum," came a voice from the doorway. "It is a fortunate thing that you are standing where you are, dear sir, or else I should have to call you out for dishonoring an innocent."

Evan and Alicia broke apart at the entrance of his sister and Stanton, who was feigning disapproval.

"He-e didn't dishonor me—" began Alicia, but she was interrupted by Ellen.

"Of course he did not," Ellen defended. "Stanton is merely teasing you. Although it is my dearest wish," she added with a meaningful look at her brother, "that there is more involved than a Christmas Eve kiss. Dare I hope?"

Evan took Alicia's hands in his and kissed them as he looked into her eyes and then turned to his sister. "You may. But it is early days yet."

He looked pointedly at the clock. "First, we must get the two of you well and truly leg-shackled. You will need your strength tomorrow—that is, later today—so I propose we bid farewell to the charming Lady Alicia and make our way to our beds."

The bridal pair left them alone for a private farewell.

"Until tomorrow," he said as they reluctantly broke apart.

"Tomorrow," she said with a tremulous smile. "I shall have to become accustomed to seeing you in that clerical collar. But in that white waistcoat, you are quite the most winsome gentleman I've met."

"I won't disappoint you," he promised.

***

The Blackburn carriage that carried them home had been supplied with warm robes and bricks wrapped in wool, but Evan didn't think his sister and her fiancé felt the cold, as wrapped up as they were in each other. But they were polite enough not to ignore Evan, although he was certain they wished him to Hades.

He inquired about the earl's health, and the pair exchanged anxious looks.

"My father is determined to see us wed," Stanton answered. "But it is a fortunate thing that the day has arrived. We were not sure but that we should have to use the special license had he taken a turn for the worst, but he has managed to endure."

Ellen squeezed his hand under the robes.

"It is well that both of you will be staying the night at Blackburn Court," Stanton continued. "In case something happens. And that your curate has agreed to do the Christmas service. That is an important day for a vicar, I should imagine."

"They have all been invited to the wedding breakfast," Ellen explained. "The prospect of being the guest of an earl has its own special charm."

"Not to mention the cachet it will give them to be able to call themselves friends of a countess," Evan teased.

"A countess." Ellen's voice wavered. "How shall I ever manage? Milton, I can't possibly..."

"Of course you can," her fiancé said with a teasing smile. "Although perhaps you might love me better if I were a dustman."

She rolled her eyes. "A dustman. Out of the question. Now a banker or solicitor, on the other hand... *that* I could do, I think."

"My sweet, for you, I would give up my title and everything I own."

His look at his bride was so tender and loving that Evan had no doubts. And Ellen, despite her words, would.have married him as a dustman in a trice.

She giggled. "Well, as for that, you needn't give up this lovely carriage. It is much more agreeable than my brother's wagon on a cold winter night."

It was indeed, thought Evan, with a sinking stomach at the reminder of his humble circumstances. How could he possibly offer a duke's daughter nothing more than a pony cart for transportation? Or bring her to a small cottage where she would have no more than one servant to help with the cooking and housekeeping?

Somehow, the magic of the evening began to wane.

Chapter Nine

25 December 1817
Blackburn Court

"That should do it," Alicia said as she attached the Blackburn tiara to Ellen's hair. "It won't fall off unless you shake your head quite vehemently, and I hardly think that will happen."

"So lovely," breathed the lady's maid who had been employed for the new viscountess.

"It *is* a lovely piece," said Ellen reverently.

The magnificent ruby in the center was surrounded by rows of diamonds and emeralds, all set in gold.

"So appropriate for a Christmas wedding."

"Indeed, but I believe Jones was speaking of you. *In* the dress. *Wearing* the tiara. Not to mention the sparkle in your eyes whenever you're thinking of your bridegroom."

Ellen blushed. "I can scarcely believe I shall soon be Milton's wife. I should never have believed... It all happened so quickly! And yet... I have no doubts. Particularly not since your feelings were not wounded in the process."

She looked up at Alicia in the dressing table mirror.

"I did worry a great deal about that, you know. Before you released him from the betrothal."

"Never mind that. Anyone who saw you together would know that you are the one for Milton. And he for you. And we never loved each other in that way. I suppose I took him for granted. And since I hadn't met anyone I liked better—well, it just seemed like the thing to do."

Alicia's heart raced as her thoughts turned to Evan. How she wished *she* could be the bride strolling up the aisle toward him, eagerly anticipating their lives together. The wedding details—the number of guests, the elaborate decorations, the gifts, even the dress—didn't matter, so long as Evan was waiting for her at the altar.

Ellen tilted her head to study Alicia. "How is it possible that you had three seasons in London, met earls and dukes and even the Prince Regent—and still had no special feeling for any of them? Were you thinking of Milton instead of taking anyone else seriously? Because if so—" She bit her lip.

Alicia giggled. "Well, the Prince Regent is married, of course. If you call *that* a marriage. But I should not wish to be a princess, in any case. I should think it rather boring being on one's best behavior day after day. As for the rest, I don't really know. I suppose I found them rather shallow. And silly. Imagine someone writing a poem to compliment my ears, as Lord Ewing did!"

They both laughed, and Alicia, in a more serious mien, added, "And I suppose I always had it in mind that my popularity came more from being a wealthy duke's daughter than my own appeal. At least I knew that would not factor in a marriage with Milton, since he has both a title *and* a fortune."

She shrugged. "But then... I tend to be rather shallow myself. Perhaps I could have made a reasonable match there."

Ellen gave an impatient sigh. "You must stop this sort of talk, my dear. Whatever you are, it is *not* shallow. Do not forget that I have seen you learning to make biscuits in the kitchen and discussing estate management with Milton. And as for accompanying my brother in visiting the poor... he says you were most gracious and not at all put off by their living conditions."

Alicia felt her face grow hot. Evan had said that about her?

"Oh well," she said in a weakened voice, "I *was* put off. Who wouldn't be? But one must be diplomatic to survive in society, so I suppose I have developed at least *some* sangfroid."

"You blush rather charmingly when you speak of my brother," Ellen said, turning in her chair to look at Alicia directly. "Does that mean you really have... special feelings for him?"

Alicia bit her lip. "Is it that obvious?"

Ellen laughed. "To anyone who knows you, yes. And I've seen the way Evan looks at you. Is there any chance you might consent to be a vicar's wife, my dear?"

Alicia's hands tingled through her gloves. "Yes, absolutely," she said with a secret small smile. "I'm not sure I should be a good one, however. My training has not extended to that, but I am willing to learn."

Ellen clapped her hands together in delight. "If you love my brother, that is all that matters." She rose and embraced Alicia. "How I should love having you as a sister! And knowing that I am not abandoning Evan to a life of solitude. I *have* been concerned that he might end up marrying that silly girl of the Greens, and I know he'd never be happy with *her*."

Alicia's misted. "Although he'd undoubtedly be better fed."

Ellen gave her a playful slap on the wrist. "Anyone can learn to cook. As a matter of fact, there's no reason Evan can't learn as well. And you'll have household help, of course."

"Oh, shall I? I wasn't sure his living could stand the expense." Alicia's relief was palpable.

Ellen shrugged. "It can't, really. But I'm sure your father will help... unless you think he might not approve..."

Alicia's throat went dry. Surely her father would not refuse his approval? Although he would be rather surprised by her choice.

"No matter," she said with a lump in her throat. "I have some money of my own that my grandmother left me."

They stared at each other. Ellen gave a small smile. "Never mind. It will all work out. I'm sure of it."

Alicia swallowed. "Of course." Then, "Let us go, shall we? I believe they are all waiting for us."

***

Evan pasted a smile on his face and entered the drawing room where Ellen was waiting.

"The earl has just been seated, and the musicians have begun the prelude. Come, my dear. The time has come for me to give you away."

He offered his arm to Ellen, and she stepped forward bravely and linked hers with his.

"That's my brother," she said fondly. "Both giving me away and officiating at the wedding." She swallowed. "How fortunate that the wedding is so small. I can't imagine why I feel so anxious with only Milton and his father and the Huntingdons in attendance."

Alicia came up from behind and hugged Ellen to her. "Never mind us. It's just you and Milton joining your lives together. It is our privilege to witness it."

She pulled back and smoothed Ellen's skirts. "There. Perfect. I shall go sit with my parents and look forward to seeing the expression on everyone's faces when they see you in your finery. Especially Milton's."

She smiled, but Evan thought there was something evasive about her glance at him. Perhaps his own second thoughts were showing in his expression. He tried to ignore the hollowness in his chest. It was Ellen's wedding day. He owed her his full attention.

The ceremony was being held in the blue drawing room, which was beautifully decorated with holly and ivy tied with large red and gold bows. The furniture had been rearranged to allow for a small musicians' gallery in the back corner and two rows of chairs covered in white cloth and decorated with colorful flowers from the Blackburn hothouse. Stanton was a magnificent bridegroom, standing tall and proud in his well-cut trousers and embroidered waistcoat from Weston.

They all rose as he and Ellen approached, except for the earl, who was grinning from ear to ear despite his obvious ill health. He caught a glimpse of the nurse eyeing her charge anxiously from the back of the room. It was believed that he was holding on to life by a thread, eager to see his son wed before succumbing. But as frail as the man appeared, Evan wondered if it might be something of an exaggeration, since he was dressed to the nines, sitting up on his own and wearing such a huge smile.

When they reached the "altar," which was a small table covered in green with two candles and a large Bible—undoubtedly the Gardiner family Bible—Evan kissed his sister on the cheek and placed her hand in Stanton's, marveling at the look of love and faith in their eyes as they gazed at each other. His Ellen was a most fortunate woman—and her bridegroom even more so. He hazarded a glance at Alicia and thought he saw her eyes glistening. Tears? Of happiness or something else? He swallowed and tried to chase away the image of sharing such a special look with her at a future wedding ceremony. Theirs.

He took his place at the altar and welcomed the guests to the ceremony. Then he turned to the Scriptures and read the famous passage from the Book of Ruth:

"And Ruth said, Entreat me not to leave thee, or to return from following after thee: for whither thou goest, I will go; and where thou lodgest, I will lodge: thy people shall be my people, and thy God my God:

Where thou diest, will I die, and there will I be buried: the Lord do so to me, and more also, if aught but death part thee and me.

When she saw that she was steadfastly minded to go with her, then she left speaking unto her."

"Here were three women, all widows in Moab with no home and no source of support. Naomi, the mother-in-law, decided to return to her native land in Bethlehem where she no doubt still had family, and she urged her daughters by marriage to return to their own families. One of them—Orpah—chose to do that. The other, Ruth, refused to abandon her beloved mother-in-law and vowed to accompany her to Israel and adapt to her customs and religion."

He turned to Ellen. "Such was the love my sister had for me that she supported me and followed me when I accepted the call to the Church. She is a true treasure to all of us fortunate enough to know her. I suppose I should be sorry to lose her, but instead, I am delighted that her sacrifice, like Ruth's, has resulted in the discovery of a loving husband who—I trust—will honor and love her for the rest of their days."

"And children!" the earl piped up with a surprisingly robust voice. "Lots of 'em!"

The guests tittered while the bridal couple smiled at each other, the bride's face flushed.

"Indeed!" pronounced Evan.

The brief wedding service which he had performed a dozen times before had never felt more meaningful and alive. *Well, of course. It's my own sister's wedding.* But as much as he tried to avoid peering at Alicia, he found himself doing so quite often. Particularly at the end when he recited the age-old homily:

"But from the beginning of the creation God made them male and female.

For this cause shall a man leave his father and mother, and cleave to his wife;

And they twain shall be one flesh: so then they are no more twain, but one flesh.

What therefore God hath joined together, let not man put asunder."

"Your Lordship—or shall I call you Brother?—you may kiss the bride."

Stanton placed his hands on Ellen's shoulders and drew her gently to him before bending his head to hers. Then they turned to face the guests, their happiness visible to all.

"Ladies and gentlemen, I present to you for the first time Lord and Lady Stanton."

* * *

Tears poured down Alicia's face, and her father handed her a handkerchief, pointing his head to his wife on his other side, whose handkerchief was already soaked.

"Women," he said softly, the sparkle in his eyes belying his complaint. "Always get emotional at weddings."

He gave her an assessing look. "I trust those *are* tears of happiness, Daughter? Not regretting the past at all?"

Alicia shook her head. "Oh no, Papa! Nothing like that! I'm just happy that they found each other."

But she couldn't help looking longingly at Evan, and was perplexed when he immediately looked away, as though he didn't wish to be caught staring at her. She flinched enough for her father to notice and ask if something was wrong.

"Oh no, of course not, Papa. I am well. Perhaps it is just a bit chilly in here."

The room was toasty from the fire, so her father frowned and drew his eyebrows together, as though he were concerned for her health.

Alicia had a premonition that the sudden chill in her heart came from the fear it would soon be broken. Because Evan didn't look like a man in love about to ask her father for permission to court her.

He's had second thoughts. I know he loves me, but does he love me enough to ignore his pride?

He was no fortune hunter, but certainly others would believe him to be one. And that was a lot to ask a gentleman to ignore.

***

The ballroom at Blackburn Court was draped in green fabric embellished with red bows and gold stars and cutouts with the initials M and E connected by a large heart. A life-size nativity scene at the far end trumpeted the primary significance of the day. But by far the greatest center of attention for the many wedding breakfast guests was the enormous table in the adjoining room that was groaning with roast goose, ham, beef, puddings, chestnut stuffing, roasted chestnuts and parsnips, bread sauce, and all sorts of cakes and biscuits.

Evan saw Alicia bustling around giving orders to the staff and looking quite lovely. Not at all the spoiled and selfish heiress she believed herself to be. It was exceedingly kind of her to offer to serve as mistress of the Court for Ellen's wedding breakfast. It was clear that she was born to be a great lady. Not one such as the stuffy Princess Lieven or any of the other pretentious Patronesses of Almack's. Alicia greeted the tenants and villagers with the same grace as the Baroness Dixon from Castle Acre and the eccentric Lady Phoenicia, a widowed relative of the Gardiners who lived in a small house in King's Lynn at the earl's expense. Occasionally she threw a questioning look at Evan and he knew she was confused by his avoidance. She must be wondering when he would approach her father. His feelings were so contradictory that he didn't know what to say to her.

I love you, but... I'm poor as a church mouse. You deserve better than the humble life of a vicar's wife. I can't give you what you deserve. I love you but... I want to be able to support my wife. I'm too proud to live on handouts from your father.

He didn't like the sound of any of them. And the thought of seeing the heartbreak in her eyes when he said them was only slightly less painful than the thought of letting her go to some other man.

And so he made his way around the room, greeting the guests and pointing them to the wassail table, which was by far the most popular spot in the room. Whenever he sensed that Alicia was moving toward him, he casually moved in the opposite direction. Finally she stopped trying, and he felt like a blackguard.

All was in vain, though, because when it was time for the bridal couple to dine, he was seated next to Alicia, who gave him a cool glare as she was seated, with her father and stepmother across the table. The duke was in a loquacious mood, having partaken liberally of the champagne that was used to toast the newlyweds, and after exclaiming over the sublime roast goose, he seemed to notice that his daughter was unusually quiet.

"Alicia, my dear, your aunt is over the moon elated about your upcoming trip to Paris. I have to confess I nearly went into apoplexy when I saw the amount she wants to spend on your wardrobe. Those Paris modistes certainly do not come cheaply!"

Alicia's mouth fell open. "But Papa..."

Her stepmother nudged her husband in the side. "Huntingdon! I simply shan't allow you to make a fuss about the cost. It's so crass to discuss money, and in any case, she must be dressed properly if she is to find a suitable match among the French. They wouldn't look at her twice dressed as she is now."

Alicia flinched.

The duke jerked his head back in surprise and glared at his wife. She swallowed and tried to apologize. "Oh dear, I didn't mean... Dear Alicia, do pardon me. I only meant that French fashion is so far more advanced than ours... Your gown is quite lovely, really. Just right for a small country wedding."

Evan clenched his teeth. Now the duchess was putting down his sister's wedding. He could easily see why Alicia had taken her in dislike. What he couldn't understand was how the duke had been taken in.

But Alicia did not take the opportunity to retaliate. "It *was* a lovely wedding, wasn't it, your grace? I vow I have never seen a more lovely ceremony."

"No. I mean, yes, it was quite affecting," the duchess replied in a subdued tone after another meaningful glance from her husband.

"Thank you, your grace," Ellen replied coolly. "We are honored that you could attend."

Then she turned to Alicia and demanded, "What is this about Paris, Alicia? Why have you not mentioned it before? I must know every detail!"

Alicia turned a pleading face to Stanton, and he covered his wife's hand with his. "There will be plenty of time for that later, my dear. Let us finish our dinner and continue our celebration."

Ellen turned to look at him and kissed him gently on the cheek.

When the evening was over, Evan realized that the only conversation between Alicia and him—besides the normal pleasantries—was when she complimented him on his fine white waistcoat. She turned away before he could return the favor, and he returned to his room that night in utter misery, anticipating the unpleasantness that was to come the next day, when he and Alicia were scheduled to distribute the Boxing Day food packages. There was guilt, yes, but also a bit of outrage, that she had led him to believe she would accept his offer of courtship when all the time she was planning a trip to Paris. Well, let her go, then. Perhaps she *would* find a suitable match.

But it didn't make him feel any less despondent to think so.

* * *

On the journey back to Huntingdon Manor, Alicia was silent as her stepmother chatted on and on about the wedding, the food, the impropriety of admitting the "great unwashed" to the manor and how the syllabub had upset her stomach.

The duke seemed to listen to her chatter in silence, although he did chuckle and call into question the reason for the upset stomach, suggesting that he was the one who should be blamed for that.

But when they walked into the front hall and handed their wraps to the butler, he told his wife that he would be up soon to bid her good night, but that he wished to speak to his daughter for a moment. In his study.

"Oh Lucas, you really must not be niggardly about the cost of her Paris wardrobe. It will be money well spent so long as she finds a husband."

The duke rolled his eyes at Alicia, and she was tempted to laugh. Elise was what she was. Alicia knew her father well enough to know that it wasn't the money that concerned him. He had pots of it. And look what it got him—a silly wife who would never in any length of time become the partner and helpmeet his first wife had been.

But what *did* he wish to speak to her about?

He came to the point immediately.

"Something is bothering you, my dear," he said, pulling up a chair across from her after she had settled down on a black leather wingback. "If it's not the loss of Milton, then what *is* it?"

He patted her knee and caught her gaze. "You are my daughter, Alicia, and even more, you are your mother's daughter. I've been watching you closely during the past few weeks, and there were times that you've seemed very happy, more so even than before Milton surprised us with his new bride. So I assumed it was true that you were not disappointed at losing him. Especially after you and Miss Campbell—that is, Lady Stanton—hit it off so well. But now… I'm not sure what is going on with you, and it concerns me greatly."

Alicia looked at her father in a blur of tears.

"Oh Papa! It's not that. It's… someone else!"

Her father rubbed his chin. "Someone else? But who…?" His eyes widened. "Campbell? You've fallen for the vicar?"

Her red eyes told him the truth.

He stiffened. "To be sure, he's an attractive fellow. But… he's a clergyman. Drives a pony cart."

Alicia looked at him with narrowed eyes.

He hastened to explain his thoughts. "Well, of course you knew that. But... have you considered what it would mean to become a vicar's wife?"

Alicia gave an impatient sigh. "If my own father doesn't believe in me, then how could anyone else? I don't know. Perhaps it *is* impossible, Father."

She told him everything—leaving out the kiss, of course. That was private. When it was all over, he rose from his seat and began pacing the room. Alicia sat in misery, her chest aching and her throat sore. Finally, he stopped pacing and pulled her out of her chair.

"First of all, I must ask your pardon for my indiscreet remark about the trip to Paris at dinner. I didn't mean to make things more difficult for you and your vicar."

Alicia closed her eyes and shook her head. "There was something else bothering him," she informed him. "He deliberately avoided me all evening. I think he might be having doubts because of—who I am."

The duke kissed her on the cheek. "Of course he is. Any man would. No one likes to be taken for a fortune hunter. And let us be frank with each other, Alicia. You have not been raised to be a country vicar's wife."

She bit her lip. "I know that. But I *have* been learning, Papa! I've learned to make tea and biscuits, and next week, Cook is planning to teach me how to make bread. And I enjoy it! These are all things that can be learned, Papa! The only thing I really care about is Evan. Being his wife."

Her father studied her and shook his head. "I don't doubt that you could. What I doubt is whether you could be happy in that sort of life. And I suspect that is what is giving your young man second thoughts as well."

He tucked his fingers under her chin to force her to look at him.

"I *have* seen a change in you, Alicia, in recent weeks. You have been kinder to your stepmother—even more than she deserves at times—and you've shown a great interest in helping those in need. Very like your mother. Damned if I don't see her in you every time I glance at you."

He pulled out a handkerchief to wipe away a tear, and then straightened up.

"I have no doubts that if you truly love this man, you'll do anything you can to have him. It won't be easy—love never is—but if this is the real thing, you'll do it."

He sighed. "But what I'm *not* certain of is how strongly he feels about you. While I certainly sympathize with his predicament—any man worth his salt expects to support his own wife—I must tell you that too many men with his pride and dignity would decline to take a wife so far superior in status and wealth."

"But... he's not a fortune hunter!"

"No, a fortune hunter would have taken you without a single qualm. He did not. Or so it appears. If he loves you enough, he'll have to let go of his pride. But there's no guarantee that he will, child. You'll have to wait until he comes to his own conclusion."

"So what do I say to him tomorrow when we take out the carriage to distribute the boxes?"

Her father pursed his lips. "Listen to your heart, my dear. Let him say his piece and respond with love. Time will tell if he has sufficient faith in your relationship to take the next step."

He folded his arms around her and held her to his chest. She hugged him back and gave him a forlorn smile.

"I suppose I can do that," she said as she pulled away to reach into her pocket to find her damp handkerchief. "But it hurts so much to think of letting him go. I know I shan't ever want to marry any other man."

Her father grinned. "Well, of course you are always welcome to remain with me and your stepmother for as long as you like."

Alicia winced. "Well, perhaps I'll become a missionary to China. I've always wished to go there, you know."

"Capital idea!" her father teased. "It certainly won't cost me the earth to dress you for the journey."

She giggled through her tears, rose to her tippy-toes and kissed him on the cheek.

But as her maid helped her out of her gown, her thoughts became morose.

I love you, Evan. Being your wife is all I care about. Please believe me. Don't leave me. But if you do, I'll wait for you. As long as it takes.

Chapter Ten

26 December 1817
East Winch, Norfolk

"Looks like a good day, weather-wise," advised the coachman as he helped Evan and the footman stack a dozen or so boxes on the backward-facing seat of the Blackburns' spacious coach. "There's room on top for the Huntingdons' boxes."

Evan shivered. "Clear sky, at least. A bit more sun would not be despised, however."

The coachman shrugged as he mounted the driver's seat. "Mebbe. It's still early."

Evan dismissed the footman and took his own seat inside the coach, giving the driver the order to depart.

He was tired after a restless night, and not at all looking forward to the inevitable conversation he would have with Alicia. His prayers to God had gone unanswered, and he still struggled to understand his own mind. It was all his fault, of course, Alicia's Paris trip notwithstanding. He should have had more self-control that night than to allow himself to lead her on, to kiss her and make promises that he might not be able to keep.

He *was* only human, however. What man in love could resist such temptation when realizing his beloved returned his feelings? *But you are a man of God. More is expected of you than the average man. If you had been in close fellowship with the Lord, you would not have fallen.*

The old insecurities had come on with a vengeance. Perhaps he had turned to the ministry as an act of contrition for his past misdeeds, and this was God's way of leading him in some other direction. Perhaps what he had taken for the "call" was merely an unconscious scheme to keep him from exposure to his old lifestyle.

It had been real enough to him at the time, though. The bishop he'd gone to for counseling had advised him to follow his inclinations and see where it led him, past or no past. He'd done so, and that's how he'd ended up at the parish in Castle Acre. With Ellen to support him. Often it seemed as though she had more faith than he.

But now she was gone, moved on to another sort of life, and he found himself at a crossroads. Remain in the ministry... alone? Marry Alicia and ignore his dignity? Or... was there another alternative?

He didn't know. And that alone was enough reason to set Alicia free. For his sake and for hers.

* * *

"Mr. Campbell is here with the Blackburn carriage, Lady Alicia," the butler informed her as she lingered at the breakfast table.

"Yes, thank you, Cooper," she said as she took a final sip of tea. "Have someone assist him with the boxes, won't you? I shall be along directly."

She shivered as she rose from her chair and checked her appearance in the hall mirror. Perfectly well-groomed, but her eyes were moist and dull and her shoulders drooped.

At least they aren't red from crying.

She'd spent the night mourning, not crying. Tears never did any good. She knew Evan was going to let her go and there was nothing she could do about it. She couldn't help being a duke's daughter. She couldn't change the fact that she had not been raised to cook or clean or lead women's groups like a vicar's wife would. Most of all, she couldn't change the fact that she had money and he didn't. If that was enough to turn him against her, then he didn't love her. Not enough.

Thus... the mourning. For a love that perhaps was never meant to be.

The butler helped her with her fur-lined wool cape.

"Oh, not the muff, Cooper. The knitted gloves will be best, I think." When you were visiting the lower classes, it was best to not to boast unduly of your own superior circumstances. At least she thought so.

When her coat and hood were fastened, Cooper opened the front door for her and stepped aside while she strode over the threshold.

The footman and the coachman were just hauling the last box to the top of the coach as she reached them. Evan turned, removed his hat, and bowed, his expression polite.

"Good morning, Lady Alicia. The air is rather chilly today. Do you think you will be warm enough?"

Her hands clenched under the cape. "I believe I am, sir. Shall we be on our way? I believe we should begin with the Smiths; they reside to the far west of Huntingdon Manor. And then we can move eastward until we reach Blackburn Court."

He nodded and gave her his arm as she ascended the steps into the carriage.

"An excellent plan. I have the list of Blackburn tenants and a general description of their locations. Are you familiar with them, your ladyship?"

"I believe so." Her tone was clipped. "I believe there's one new family I haven't met yet, but I can direct you to their home. I have been assisting Milton on Boxing Day for many years now."

After they had seated themselves as far away as possible from each other on the forward-facing seat, Evan gave the order and the coach rolled on its way.

Other than a few comments about the wedding, the coach was silent most of the way to the first stop. Alicia stared out of the window and Evan appeared to be concentrating on the Blackburn boxes on the opposite seat.

Mr. and Mrs. Kirk were thirty-ish and their two-year-old daughter was the light of their lives. Alicia knew their first child had been stillborn and Mrs. Kirk seemed to have trouble conceiving. She could well remember their grief from the loss of the first and their fears that they might never be blessed with a child. Now that they had Jane, their anxiety seemed to have disappeared.

Clara Kirk, with the toddler on her hip, greeted them enthusiastically and invited them into the small, but neat cottage.

"My husband will wish ta speak to ye before ye go. He went out ta feed the animals and milk the cows, but he should be back directly."

She seated them by the fire and offered them tea, which they refused, with the comment that they were disbursing boxes for the Blackburns as well the Huntingdons and had a heavy schedule for the day.

"A pleasure to meet ye, Mr. Campbell," she said, pausing to examine him. "Felicitations on yer sister's fine weddin'. A lovely bride, she was. Twas a grand weddin' breakfast too. Such a privilege ta be invited."

Evan thanked her, and she turned her attention to Alicia and inquired as to her stepmother's health.

"Her Grace is well enough," Alicia responded. "She is in the family way again, however, and quite queasy in the mornings, so my offer to replace her today was very well received."

Clara Kirk's face lit up. "What a blessin' that is! The young master will have a young brother or sister to play with. My Jane's ta have one as well, ye know." She patted her stomach. "In May." She beamed at Evan. "The Lord is good, sir."

"Indeed he is, Mrs. Kirk."

But his smile seemed forced.

The door opened and a dark bearded man, tall and stocky, filled the doorway. Clara put down her child to greet him and perform the introductions. Little Jane toddled over to Alicia, sucking her thumb and looking up hopefully.

Alicia pulled her onto her lap and gave her a big hug. "Hello, Jane. My, have you grown! You have such pretty eyes, you know. Did you know that?"

Jane's response was to nod enthusiastically and continue to suck her thumb while studying Alicia intently.

Alicia kissed the child's silky soft hair and bounced her on her knee as she did with her little brother. The thumb came out and the girl burst into delighted giggles.

"She likes ye." Bert Kirk entered the circle and beamed with pride at his daughter. "Senses ye like young 'uns. Not everbody does, ye know."

He looked pointedly at Evan. "What about ye, Vicar? Figurin' on havin' young' uns someday?"

Evan cleared his throat. "Yes, of course. If the Lord wills it."

He shifted in his chair, and Alicia wanted to laugh... if she didn't cry first. The Kirks were looking at them as though they were a couple, and it made him uncomfortable.

"His sister—the new Lady Stanton, you know—helped me prepare the boxes for both our estates, and Mr. Campbell graciously agreed to take her place in the distribution."

"Very kind of ye, sir. And your ladyship as well. We thank ye well for yer kindness."

But Bert's knowing smile persisted as the conversation turned to the wedding and the generous spread the Blackburns had provided for the neighborhood.

Finally, Evan rose and announced they needed to be on their way.

"Mighty kind of ye," Bert said as he scooped Rebecca out of

Alicia's lap. "Wishin' ye and her ladyship here much health and happiness in the new year."

Evan's face was frozen as he helped her into the carriage. Alicia felt it was time to break the silence.

As he sat down next to her, she drew a breath and released it before she took his hand and spoke in a soft voice.

"Evan, tell me what is wrong. I gather you've had second thoughts. Can we not at least speak about it?"

He uttered a soft, distinctly un-vicar-like curse and leaned his head back against the squabs.

Finally, he sat up and grimaced. "I-I was wrong to say-do those things to you, Alicia. I'm not fit to be your husband. Please pardon me for taking advantage. For leading you on."

Finally it was all out in the open.

"I do *not* pardon you, Evan Campbell! What happened between us on Christmas Eve was *real*. It was not a cheap tryst in some dark alley. I am not a hussy and you are not a rake. We *love* each other. Can you deny it?" Chin high, she glared at him.

He turned away. "You don't know me, Alicia. Not really. In the few weeks since we met, you've come to care about a man who is nothing but a sham."

A sham? That was unexpected. Alicia tilted her head to one side.

"If you're speaking of your youth when you were carousing in London, I already know about that. Ellen told me. All young men go through that stage. Why–you've become a completely different person since then. Why let the past consume you now when you know you cannot change it?"

He pounded the wall of the carriage. "It's easy for you to say that. The worst you have done is bait your stepmother. While... I am guilty of so much more."

Alicia's heart skipped a beat. "My offenses are not so benign as you think, Evan. But if you believe yours are so unpardonable that you believe yourself unworthy, why not tell me the whole and see if I agree with your assessment?"

Evan closed his eyes and palmed his face. "My father and I fought constantly as I grew up. His greatest wish was to see me in the ministry. I wished to go abroad—India perhaps—and seek my fortune. Get away from my father's strictures and make a life for myself in London society."

He took a deep breath. "When I was eighteen he told me that he had enrolled me in the Divinity program at Oxford without my knowledge. I was livid, of course. We were still arguing when he had an attack of the heart and fell at my feet. Dead." His chin trembled.

Alicia gasped and put her arm around his shoulders. "How dreadful!"

"Afterward, I discovered that he had inherited a fortune from a Scottish relative before my sister and I were born, and he'd managed to save it—along with a significant amount of interest—for his children. Ellen and I were still underage, but the original trustee named in the will had died and his heir wiped his hands of the responsibility. And suddenly I had ten thousand pounds and the world was my oyster."

"Ten thousand pounds!" Alicia's hand flew to her chest.

Evan's hands curled tightly. "Indeed. If I had not squandered the lot, I should have enough to purchase my wife a carriage or keep servants or at the very least put some away for our children." He shook his head sadly as he met her eyes. "But no. All I knew at the time was that I had the means to make my every dream come true. Life is short, so it's best to eat, drink and be merry while one can."

"But-But- you were young and foolish," Alicia defended. "We must all learn from our mistakes. You are no longer that foolish young man."

Evan's tone deepened. "But it wasn't just that. Yes, I drank, whored, gambled, threw away my inheritance. Those things are certainly reprehensible enough. But I also deserted my ailing mother to the care of my sister."

His chin trembled. "She never lost faith in me, not once. Nor did my sister ever remonstrate with me, not once. They both supported and believed in me. Even when I returned like the Prodigal Son after I'd squandered everything, they welcomed me and brought me back to the faith."

His voice quivered. "I grew increasingly convinced that with my experience, I could be useful in helping others along their spiritual journeys, and after much reflection and consultation, I concluded that I had been called to the ministry."

He sighed heavily. "But now... I'm not certain." He shook his head as he looked at her. "How could I possibly go to your father, tell him all of this—particularly that I am seriously reconsidering my call to the ministry and have no means of supporting a wife—and then ask for your hand in marriage?"

Alicia felt a heaviness in her heart and limbs. "No, I suppose you could not, Evan. But I love you." Her voice cracked.

"I know," he said, gently touching her cheek. "I love you too. But perhaps love is not enough."

He clasped her hands in his and they sat gazing into each other's eyes until the carriage halted at their next stop.

* * *

The remainder of their Boxing Day visits passed in a blur. Alicia smiled and chatted briefly with the recipients, but her smile did not reach her eyes, and Evan thought he could detect despair in them at times when she was handed a baby or faced with a loving young couple such as the Kirks. No doubt she was envisioning the children she would never have with him, and he berated himself for being the cause of her sadness.

At one point he tried to tell her that she would forget him and marry someone more worthy, but that resulted in a slap on the face and an outburst of tears. So much for that. He was a fool to think that she could be so easily consoled.

The last tenant farm on their list was let to the Fentons, an older couple whose home had been frequented by Stanton and

Alicia when they were children. After Mrs. Fenton and Alicia's warm embrace, the latter peered into her morose eyes and shook her head sadly.

"Ye've heard, then. Poor Lord Blackburn! A fine gentleman he was, and the best landlord. I'm sure young Stanton—of course, he's Blackburn now, dear heaven, I can't get my head around it—will follow in his father's footsteps."

Evan froze for a moment until he saw Alicia sway on her feet, whereupon he hastened to her side and gripped her upper arms and clasped her to his chest for support.

"The earl... has died?" He heard himself asking. "When?"

Mrs. Fenton's hands flew to her cheeks. "Oh dear. Ye didn't know, did ye? I thought for sure... or I would never—"

Her husband came forward to clasp his wife's wringing hands. "The greengrocer was just up there for a delivery and had it direct from Mrs. Berry. Seems his lordship held off until after the wedding. Went peaceful-like, so she said."

Alicia's eyes filled with tears. Seeing her shoulders shake, Evan put his arm around her to keep her steady. "I should go," he said. He was, after all, responsible for the East Winch parish in the absence of the current one. The death of such a prominent figure in the parish was a momentous event. And then there was Ellen. Only just married and now in mourning!

He glanced anxiously at the remaining boxes in the carriage. Alicia was in no condition to continue on her own.

"I'll deliver 'em for ye," Mr. Fenton offered. "I can hitch up old Nell to the wagon and get 'em out right quick."

"Thank you so much!" Alicia hugged him enthusiastically, causing his face to redden. Evan gave him the list and shook his hand. "I'm in your debt, Mr. Fenton."

Fenton clapped him on the shoulder. "Not 'tall, Vicar. The Lord be with ye."

Chapter Eleven

1818
Alicia

In the end, she had gone to Paris after all. She saw the cathedral of Notre Dame, still damaged from the Revolution, the jewel-like windows of the Sainte Chapelle, the magnificence of the Church of Les Invalides, and the Louvre Museum. She strolled down the Champs-Élysées, saw the wooden version of Arc de Triomphe in the center of the Place de l'Étoile, promenaded in the Gardens of the Tuileries, Luxembourg, and Plants, and viewed the magnificent city from the Pont Neuf. Magnificent, yes, but one didn't have to look far to see the ravages of war. The Place de la Concorde near where a thousand people lost their lives with the drop of a blade. She and Aunt Beatrice were safely installed in the Hotel Westminster when someone tried to assassinate the Duke of Wellington, but that failed attempt was not the first time she felt unwelcome—and unsafe to a certain extent—in the city. Too many French citizens looked upon the English with suspicion as they walked the streets, even as they accepted their coins and custom. Alicia wished she had not agreed to come.

But Aunt Beatrice had insisted, and with nothing else to do, she had finally accepted. Milton and Ellen were in deep mourning, and although she was always welcome at Blackburn Court, Evan was often there, and even if he was not, the conversation almost always included him, and Alicia found that painful. Did he still love her? Was he courting some other woman, one more suited to be a vicar's wife? While that particular subject never came up in conversation, she couldn't erase it from her thoughts.

Evan Campbell had come to speak to her father on New Year's Day; he was the First Foot, actually. Good fortune for the coming year. Perhaps a wedding? But alas, that was not to be. At least not yet. He and the duke spent well over an hour in the duke's study, and when the door finally opened, Evan emerged, his head down until he spotted her on the stairs.

"My dear Alicia," he said as she rushed into his arms.

"What happened? What did Papa say?"

"Never fear, my love. He will not stand in our way. But he suggested—and I agree—that we not rush into marriage until we are both certain that this is what we both want."

"I'm certain! Aren't you, Evan?"

"I know I love you, Alicia."

"And I love you!" she cried. "What else is there? Nothing that matters."

He grimaced. "Perhaps not. But don't you see—it's too soon, Alicia. We've known each other a matter of weeks. We were raised so differently, you and I. I have to know that you won't regret giving up a life of luxury to live in a vicarage."

"But I can! I know I can! I don't care about those things!" Her eyes filled with tears and her body began to sway. He half carried her to the stairs and set her down, holding her in his arms as he sat down beside her.

"Of course you don't. But your father and I believe that a few months apart will only strengthen the feelings we have for each other, if they are true."

She looked up at him, searching his eyes. "A few months? But

Evan —what shall we do?" The pit in her stomach seemed to expand exponentially at every word coming out of his mouth.

"I go about my business as usual, and you—do what you've always done. The London Season. Resume your place as the Belle of the Ball, this time without a betrothal to deter the beaux." She punched his arm. "Do not be mistaken. If you fall for another fellow I shall be devastated, but it's your happiness I wish for, my love. If you return determined to live your life as a humble vicar's wife, I shall be the happiest man on earth."

"I shan't enjoy a moment of it." Then she tilted her head as she studied him. "What about you? I can't promise to dance at your wedding if you find another woman to love."

"Well," he said as he pretended to consider it, "I can't think I shall meet anyone like you, my dear. On the other hand, Mrs. Green's daughter makes a fine rabbit stew."

So she went to Paris and danced with bankrupt *comtes* and *ducs*, soldiers of many nationalities, and even the Duc de Richelieu himself, in golden ballrooms with crystal chandeliers and priceless paintings and art. It all seemed excessive to her, as though everyone there were trying to prove they were happy with their extravagant lives. It wasn't *real*. These people had so recently been at war with one another, causing great suffering and tragedy for so many, and now they paraded ballrooms in costly silks and satins in an endless attempt to find pleasure.

But she was still Alicia and couldn't resist having a few dresses made up for the upcoming Season. Perhaps not as many as she might have done before she'd fallen in love with a clergyman. One of them was a simple white round gown of gauze, with a satin overdress, and blond lace around the short waist. Her aunt commented that it could have passed as a wedding gown, but Alicia refused to comment.

The London Season had a very different ambience for Alicia. The news of her broken betrothal had the effect of nearly all of the eligible gentlemen stalking her like prey. As for the ladies, well, for the first time Alicia knew what it was like to be the subject of idle talk and gossip.

"So sorry to hear about Blackburn, my dear. A man like that doesn't like to be taken for granted."

"I hear he married a clergyman's sister. So humiliating for you."

"So you didn't find a penniless *comte* to marry in Paris? I hear they can be found on every street corner."

Some were more sympathetic, of course. She was still a wealthy duke's daughter. But they too would ridicule her when they heard she'd married a vicar. A part of her felt sad that she'd wasted so many years—well, five now since she'd come out—flitting about with superficial people with nothing to do but indulge their every whim and look down their noses at those less fortunate than they were. As she had been at the time.

London Society wasn't *all* superficial, however. She attended a musical evening at the Foundling Hospital, returning the next day to visit the children, where she felt her heart would break at the thought of having to abandon a child of her own. *She* wouldn't have to, of course. But it felt so wrong that any mother should have to do so. These children were fed and clothed and given a basic education before setting out to become a servant or an apprentice, but what happened to those whose application to the Hospital was denied? It hardly bore thinking about. Alicia knew the power of prayer, but she felt more than prayer was required to right these wrongs. She made a donation and determined to discuss this with Evan as soon as she saw him again.

Evan! She missed him so much! No society gentleman could measure up to him. They weren't all fortune hunters, but they seemed so *shallow* to her now. Well, they weren't all wastrels. Lord Symington, just out of mourning for his first wife, was said to be a kind, honest man devoted to his estate who needed a wife and mother for his four children. They talked across the dinner table once and got along famously, but there was no romantic connection there, and his wasn't one of the dozens of bouquets that crowded the hall tables every morning.

At times she wanted to shake sense into her father for suggesting they spend time apart—and do the same to Evan for agreeing with him. Why couldn't they see that she was no longer the silly girl she had been last year when she'd been sent away from London in disgrace? She'd even called on the new Duchess of Aylesbury when she'd first arrived in town, to apologize for her rudeness last year when the as yet unmarried Rebecca had caused her to spill wine on her ivory taffeta gown.

"It was an accident, of course," she explained. "There was *such* a crush at that ball. It could have happened to anyone."

"But your dress was ruined!" Rebecca exclaimed. "You were right to be annoyed. Anyone would be!"

"Oh, I don't think so, your grace. I don't think *you* would have reacted in such a way. I had a roomful of dresses and still do, more's the pity. What shall I do with them when I marry a clergyman?"

Rebecca shook her head, no doubt still finding it hard to believe that her former tormenter had changed so much in the past year that she was set to marry a man of the cloth. "Well, perhaps you might keep some," she suggested.

Alicia bit her lip. "I might do, at least a few. You see, I have a plan to hold charity balls at my father's house in London. For worthy charities, of course. But nobody needs as many frilly gowns as I have. Perhaps I shall sell some of them and donate the funds to the parish poor."

The duchess studied her intently. "I believe you are really sincere. Your clergyman has worked wonders, it appears."

Alicia gave a wry smile. "Yes indeed, along with a liberal dose of humility, and the grace of God." She set her teacup down on the nearby table. "I wasn't raised to be so shallow, not while my mother was alive. After she died, I had no one to check me—Papa was unequal to the task—and my behavior got quite out of hand." A flush crept across her face. "I also want to apologize for what I said about you needing to hold back on the bonbons. You weren't at all fat, just a bit—er—fuller than most, and it was cruel of me to point it out."

Her Grace burst out laughing. "I'm sorry," she said, wiping her eyes with her handkerchief. "It's just that you see me now much fuller at present than I was at the time." She rested her hands on the noticeable bump popping out from underneath her morning gown.

Alicia laughed as well. "It appears that Aylesbury found your proportions most pleasing. When is the new addition to arrive?"

"Mid-July. I expect to be confined before May, and Miles will return here until Parliament is dissolved. He would prefer to stay with me in the country, but my mother and sister will be there, and the government is in such disarray that he really can't abandon them."

So the two ladies enjoyed their tea together, talking mostly babies, Alicia mentioning her half-brother Gervase and the half-sibling due around the same time as Rebecca's.

She couldn't help hoping that next year might find *her* in the family way. Please God!

* * *

1818
Evan

Life as the Vicar of Castle Acre Parish continued at a slower pace once the regular vicar at the neighboring parish returned to his duties after the holidays. He was grateful for the assistance Evan had lent to his curate in his absence and offered to return the favor at some time in the future. That might come in useful, Evan thought, so that he and Alicia could have a honeymoon.

Providing there *was* a honeymoon. And a wedding first, of course. Unfortunately, Evan had a great deal more time on his hands, with Ellen gone to live with her husband. He had a local woman in to clean and do his shopping, and she left a stew or a roast on the fire for his dinner. Celia Green found a suitor and lost interest in him, but the church ladies kept him stocked up with bread and meat pies and biscuits for tea. Not knowing his connection with the duke's daughter, plenty of mothers extolled the virtues of their unmarried daughters, but he was careful to show them no more attention than he did his other parishioners.

He was often a visitor at Blackburn Court, still shrouded in mourning for the previous earl. They had elected to postpone Milton's introduction to the House of Lords until the next opening of Parliament, and Evan thought this a wise decision for the newly married couple. The delay gave Ellen more time to adjust to her new rank before being thrust on Society, and it also functioned as an extended honeymoon. Evan was happy for them, but at times, their secret smiles and private looks seemed too much to bear. Especially since they had been able to marry so quickly and not been constrained to wait.

Yes, there were times when he was overcome by resentment, by fear that he would lose Alicia to some man more suitable to be her husband. He tried to convince himself that it was her happiness he wanted more than anything else, but he wasn't sure that was true. Would God give him this love and then take it away? And if He did, would that be enough to drag him back to the old darkness? He prayed for strength.

And then there were times when he sat with married couples who had come to dislike, even hate, each other. He counseled them as best he could, but for many there wasn't much he could do. He couldn't stop Old Bates from drinking, and Mrs. Bates had to stay to protect the children. There really needed to be some sort of respite for women in this position. Perhaps Alicia could help him find a solution. Surely the two of them could manage it.

Just before Lent, Evan was stunned when an old crony of his came to call. A squire's son from the next county who'd been among his companions back in his carousing days. Only Leonard no longer seemed to have the *joie de vivre* he'd had in the past.

"Why Leonard, what a surprise—that is, I'm so glad to see you again." It was one of those little white lies he thought God would understand. In truth, Evan didn't like to be reminded of the old days when he'd ruined his life. Or tried to, at least. "Come in, come in. I can get you some tea."

Leonard smiled briefly. It didn't reach his eyes, however. "No Mrs. Campbell yet?"

Evan bit his lip. "Not yet." He led his former friend into the study and urged him to sit down while he went to the kitchen. After a few minutes, he returned with the tea tray and poured them each a cup.

"So very domesticated you have become, my friend. And biscuits as well."

They drank and ate in silence, and finally Leonard came to the point of his visit.

"I've made a mess of my life, Evan, and you're the only one I know who's managed to make it out of the snake pit. Felham is in debtors' prison, you know. And Potts shot himself. The others are in varying degrees of misery. Including me."

"But you're here and they are not. What can I do for you, my friend?"

And so began the story of Leonard's misspent youth. Not all of it was new to Evan, since he'd played a part in it himself, but Leonard had managed to make a mess of his marriage as well. His father had discovered a village girl had fallen pregnant by him and demanded he wed her or be disinherited in favor of his cousin. So he did the easy thing and married the girl. And proceeded to make her life a living hell.

He didn't have to explain further; Evan understood quite well how such things happened. He clapped a hand on his friend's shoulder. "What can I do for you, my friend?"

"I want to make it up to her," he said in an emotion-choked voice. "I want to be worthy of her trust. A good father for my son. But... I don't know how. I've been such a beast to her. I don't deserve to be forgiven."

"Ah," said Evan, "you must first forgive yourself, my friend."

And that was when he became aware that he, too, had never really forgiven himself. Ellen had tried to tell him, but all he could think was that she didn't know how far he had fallen. He'd become a clergyman as a way of atoning for his sins of the past. Helping others instead of hurting them. But it never was *enough*, was it? It weighed on his mind every hour of every day, and he was always thinking that if others knew the real Evan, they'd know he didn't deserve to be their vicar. He didn't deserve to be happy. He didn't deserve to be Alicia's husband.

"If we confess our sins, he is faithful and just to forgive our sins and cleanse us from all unrighteousness."

After the two of them had prayed together, they spent the remainder of the afternoon talking and counseling each other, and after Leonard's departure, Evan felt a lightness in his chest he hadn't felt before.

And he couldn't wait to tell Alicia all about it.

Chapter Twelve

24 December 1818
East Winch Parish Church

"Now that Alicia and Evan have given themselves to each other by solemn vows, with the joining of hands and the giving and receiving of a ring, I pronounce that they are husband and wife, in the Name of the Father, and of the Son, and of the Holy Spirit. Those whom God has joined together let no one put asunder."

The Reverend Wilkes smiled broadly as the bride and groom turned to face the wedding guests, packed into every nook and cranny of the church, who clapped and cheered loudly as the newly married couple turned their heads to the side and kissed.

Alicia wore her elegant white gown from Paris, her mother's veil, and a bouquet of flowers in shades of red, gold, and white for the holidays. Evan wore the white waistcoat he'd worn at Ellen and Milton's wedding, but with a new pair of ivory trousers and a charcoal jacket. Beaming with happiness, they strolled down the aisle, followed by Ellen and Milton, matron of honor and best man, and they all signed the register, happy tears flowing liberally down their cheeks.

Once Alicia and Evan had reunited after their months apart,

the duke had agreed to announce their engagement. Completely secure in each other's love, the couple had decided not to marry in haste, but to take time for a courtship, to discuss their future together, and, of course, plan the wedding. A Christmas wedding made sense, of course, since both Milton and the duke had responsibilities in Parliament following the general election that summer. The Blackburns' mourning would be over, and their blacks could be put aside in time to celebrate the nuptials of the happy couple. They would take their honeymoon at the duke's hunting box in Weymouth, where they could enjoy the sea views, the beaches, and the village shops. And each other, of course.

"A toast to the happy couple!" The duke raised his glass in their direction, a gleam in his eye. "And for the hope of many grandchildren to come."

His wife, sitting beside him with baby Louis in her arms, turned white with horror.

Evan and Alicia's eyes met, and they grinned.

"Let's do it," Alicia whispered. "Let's make Elise a grandmother."

"As soon as may be," Evan agreed, sealing their promise with a kiss.

About the Author

ABOUT SUSANA ELLIS

Susana Ellis is a retired teacher, part-time caregiver, sewist, cook, and fashion print collector. Lifelong reading and a fascination with history led her to writing historical romances. She is one of the original Bluestocking Belles and a member of Regency Fiction Writers and the Maumee Valley Romance Authors Inc.

SOCIAL MEDIA

You can contact Susana Ellis at these social media links:
  susanaellisauthor@gmail.com
  https://www.pinterest.com/susanaauthor
  https://susanaellisauthor.blog

About the Bluestocking Belles

The Bluestocking Belles (the "BellesInBlue") are seven very different writers united by a love of history and a history of writing about love. From sweet to steamy, from light-hearted fun to dark tortured tales full of angst, from London ballrooms to country cottages to the sultan's seraglio, one or more of us will have a tale to suit your tastes and mood.

Learn more about the Bluestocking Belles at:
Website: www.BluestockingBelles.net/
Newsletter: http://eepurl.com/dAJU_9
Teatime Tattler twice-weekly gossip magazine:
https://bluestockingbelles.net/category/teatime-tattler/
Free books: https://bluestockingbelles.net/teatime-tattler-free-books/

Made in United States
Orlando, FL
11 July 2024